Charlotte Mary Yonge

The Prince and the Page

Outlook

Charlotte Mary Yonge

The Prince and the Page

1. Auflage | ISBN: 978-3-73261-946-7

Erscheinungsort: Paderborn, Deutschland

Erscheinungsjahr: 2018

Outlook Verlag GmbH, Paderborn.

THE PRINCE AND THE PAGE

by Charlotte M. Yonge

PREFACE

In these days of exactness even a child's historical romance must point to what the French term its pieces justficatives. We own that ours do not lie very deep. The picture of Simon de Montfort drawn by his wife's own household books, as quoted by Mrs. Everett Green in her Lives of the Princesses, and that of Edward I. in Carte's History, and more recently in the Greatest of the Plantagenets, furnished the two chief influences of the story. The household accounts show that Earl Simon and Eleanor of England had five sons. Henry fell with his father at Evesham. Simon and Guy deeply injured his cause by their violence, and after holding out Kenilworth against the Prince, retired to the Continent, where they sacrilegiously murdered Henry, son of the King of the Romans—a crime so much abhorred in Italy that Dante represents himself as meeting them in torments in the Inferno, not however before Guy had become the founder of the family of the Counts of Monforte in the Maremma. Richard, the fourth son, appears in the household books as possessing dogs, and having garments bought for him; but his history has not been traced after his mother left England. The youngest son, Amaury, obtained the hereditary French possessions of the family, and continued the line of Montfort as a French subject. Eleanor, the only daughter, called the Demoiselle de Montfort, married, as is well known, the last native prince of Wales, and died after a few years.

The adventure of Edward with the outlaw of Alton Wood is one of the stock anecdotes of history, and many years ago the romance of the encounter led the author to begin a tale upon it, in which the outlaw became the protector of one of the proscribed family of Montfort. The commencement was placed in one of the manuscript magazines which are so often the amusement of a circle of friends. It was not particularly correct in its details, and the hero bore the peculiarly improbable name of Wilfred (by which he has since appeared in the Monthly Packet). The story slept for many years in MS., until further reading and thought had brought stronger interest in the period, and for better or for worse it was taken in hand again. Joinville, together with the authorities quoted by Sismondi, assisted in picturing the arrival of the English after the death of St. Louis, and the murder of Henry of Almayne is related in all crusading histories; but for Simon's further career, and for his implication in the attempt on Edward's life at Acre, the author is alone responsible, taking

1

refuge in the entire uncertainty that prevails as to the real originator of the crime, and perhaps an apology is likewise due to Dante for having reversed his doom.

For the latter part of the story, the old ballad of The Blind Beggar of Bethnal Green, gives the framework. That ballad is believed to be Elizabethan in date, and the manners therein certainly are scarcely accordant with the real thirteenth century, and still less with our notions of the days of chivalry. Some liberties therefore have been taken with it, the chief of them being that Bessee is not permitted to go forth to seek her fortune in the inn at Romford, and the readers are entreated to believe that the alteration was made by the traditions which repeated Henry de Montfort's song.

It was the late Hugh Millar who alleged that the huge stone under which Edward sleeps in Westminster Abbey agrees in structure with no rocks nearer than those whence the mighty stones of the Temple at Jerusalem were hewn, and there is no doubt that earth and stones were frequently brought by crusaders from the Holy Land with a view to the hallowing of their own tombs.

The author is well aware that this tale has all the incorrectnesses and inconsistencies that are sure to attend a historical tale; but the dream that has been pleasant to dream may be pleasant to listen to; and there can be no doubt that, in spite of all inevitable faults, this style of composition does tend to fix young people's interest and attention on the scenes it treats of, and to vivify the characters it describes; and if this sketch at all tends to prepare young people's minds to look with sympathy and appreciation on any of the great characters of our early annals, it will have done at least one work.

December 12th, 1865.

CHAPTER I—THE STATELY HUNTER

"'Now who are thou of the darksome brow
  Who wanderest here so free?'
"'Oh, I'm one that will walk the green green woods,
  Nor ever ask leave of thee.'"—S. M.

A fine evening—six centuries ago—shed a bright parting light over Alton Wood, illuminating the gray lichens that clung to the rugged trunks of the old oak trees, and shining on the smoother bark of the graceful beech, with that sidelong light that, towards evening, gives an especial charm to woodland scenery. The long shadows lay across an open green glade, narrowing towards one end, where a path, nearly lost amid dwarf furze, crested heather, and soft bent-grass, led towards a hut, rudely constructed of sods of turf and branches of trees, whose gray crackling foliage contrasted with the fresh verdure around. There was no endeavour at a window, nor chimney; but the door of wattled boughs was carefully secured by a long twisted withe.

A halbert, a broken arrow, a deer-skin pegged out on the ground to dry, a bundle of faggots, a bare and blackened patch of grass, strewn with wood ashes, were tokens of recent habitation, though the reiterations of the nightingale, the deep tones of the blackbird and the hum of insects, were the only sounds that broke the stillness.

Suddenly the silence was interrupted by a clear, loud, ringing whistle, repeated at brief intervals and now and then exchanged for the call —"Leonillo! Leon!" A footstep approached, rapidly overtaken and passed by the rushing gallop of a large animal; and there broke on the scene a large tawny hound, prancing, bounding, and turning round joyfully, pawing the air, and wagging his tail, in welcome to the figure who followed him.

This was a youth thirteen years old, wearing such a dress as was usual with foresters—namely, a garment of home-spun undyed wool, reaching to the knee, and there met by buskins of deer-skin, with the dappled hair outside; but the belt which crossed one shoulder was clasped with gold, and sustained a dagger, whose hilt and sheath were of exquisite workmanship. The cap on his head was of gray rabbit- skin, but a heron's plume waved in it; the dark curling locks beneath were carefully arranged; and the port of his head and shoulders, the mould of his limbs, the cast of his features, and the fairness of his complexion, made his appearance ill accord with the homeliness of his garb. In one hand he carried a bow over his shoulder; in the other he held by the ears a couple of dead rabbits, with which he playfully tantalized the dog, holding them to his nose, and then lifting them high aloft, while the hound, perfectly entering into the sport, leapt high after them with open mouth, and pretended to seize them, then bounded and careered round his young master with gay short barks, till both were out of breath; and the boy, flinging the rabbits on the turf, threw himself down on it, with one arm upon the neck of the panting dog, whose great gasps, like a sobbing of laughter, heaved his whole frame.

"Ay, good Leonillo, take your rest!" said the boy: "we have done yeoman's service to-day, and shown ourselves fit to earn our own livelihood! We are outlaws now, my lion of the Pyrenees; and you at least lead a merrier life than in the castle halls, when we hunted for sport, and not for sustenance! Well-a-day, my Leon!"—as the creature closed his mouth, and looked wistfully up at him with almost human sympathy and intelligence—"would that we knew where are all that were once wont to go with us to the chase! But for them, I would be well content to be a bold forester all my days! Better so, than to be ever vexed and crossed in every design for the country's weal—distrusted

4

above—betrayed beneath! Alack! alack! my noble father, why wert thou wrecked in every hope—in every aim!"

These murmurings were broken off as Leonillo suddenly crested his head, and changed his expression of repose for one of intense listening.

"Already!" exclaimed the boy, springing to his feet, as Leonillo bounded forward to meet a stout hardy forester, who was advancing from the opposite end of the glade. This was a man of the largest and most sinewy mould, his face tanned by sun and wind to a uniform hard ruddy brown, and his shaggy black hair untrimmed, as well as his dark bristly beard. His jerkin was of rough leather, crossed by a belt, sustaining sword and dagger; a bow and arrows were at his back; a huge quarter-staff in his hand; and his whole aspect was that of a ferocious outlaw, whose hand was against every man.

But the youth started towards him gleefully, as if the very sight of him had dispelled all melancholy musings, and shouted merrily, "Welcome—welcome, Adam! Why so early home? Have the Alton boors turned surly? or are the King's prickers abroad, and the neighbourhood unwholesome for bold clerks of St. Nicholas?"

"Worse!" was the gruff mutter in reply. "Down, Leon: I am in no mood for thy freaks!"

"What is it, Adam? Have the keepers carried their complaints to the King, of the venison we have consumed, with small thanks to him?"

"Prince Edward is at Alton! What think you of that, Sir? Come to seek through copse and brake for the arrant deer-stealer and outlaw, and all his gang!"

"Why, there's preferment for you!" said the boy, laughing. "High game for the heir of the throne! And his gang! Hold up your head, Leonillo: you and I come in for a share of the honour!"

"Hold up your head!" said the outlaw bitterly. "You may chance to hold it as high as your father's is, for all your gibes and jests, my young Lord, if the Longshanks gets a hold of you, which our Lady forefend."

"Nay, I think better of my Cousin Longshanks. I loved him well when I was his page at Hereford: he was tenderer to me than ever my brothers were; and I scarce think he would hang, draw, and quarter me now."

"You may try, if you are not the better guided."

"How did you hear these tidings?" inquired the boy, changing his mood to a graver one.

"From the monk to whom you confessed a fortnight back. Did you let him

5

know your lineage?"

"How could I do otherwise?"

"He looked like a man who would keep a secret; and yet—"

"Shame—shame to doubt the good father!"

"Nay, I do not say that I do; but I would have the secret in as few men's power as may be. Nevertheless, I thank the good brother. He called out to me as he saw me about to enter the town, that if I had any tenderness for my own life, I had best not show myself there; and he went on to tell me how the Prince was come to his hunting-lodge, with hawk and hound indeed, but for the following of men rather than bird or beast."

"And what would you have me do?"

"Be instantly on the way to the coast, ere the search begins; and there, either for love of Sir Simon the righteous or for that gilt knife of yours, we may get ferried over to the Isle of Wight, whence- -But what ails the dog! Whist, Leonillo! Hold your throat: I can hear naught but your clamour!"

The hound was in fact barking with a tremendous lion-like note; and when, on reiterated commands from his master and the outlaw, he changed it for a low continuous growling like distant thunder, a step and a rustling of the boughs became audible.

"They are upon us already!" cried the boy, snatching up and stringing his bow.

"Leave me to deal with him!" returned the outlaw. "Off to Alton: the good father will receive you to sanctuary!"

"Flee!—never!" cried the boy. "You teaching my father's son to flee!"

"Tush!—'tis but one!" said the outlaw. "He is easily dealt with; and he shall have no time to call his fellows."

So saying, the forester strode forward into the wood, where a tall figure was seen through the trees; and with uplifted quarter-staff, dealt a blow of sudden and deadly force as soon as the stranger came within its sweep, totally without warning. The power of the stroke might have felled an ox, and would have at once overthrown the new- comer, but that he was a man of unusual stature; and this being unperceived in the outlaw's haste, the blow lighted on his left shoulder instead of on his head.

"Ha, caitiff!" he exclaimed; and shortening the hunting-pole in his hand, he returned the stroke with interest, but the outlaw had already prepared himself to receive the blow on his staff. For some seconds there was a rapid exchange;

and all that the boy could detect in the fierce flourish of weapons was, that his champion was at least equally matched. The height of the stranger was superior; and his movements, if less quick and violent, had an equableness that showed him a thorough master of his weapon. But ere the lad had time to cross the heather to the scene of action, the fight was over; the outlaw lay stunned and motionless on the ground, and the gigantic stranger was leaning on his hunting-pole, regarding him with a grave unmoved countenance, the fair skin of which was scarcely flushed by the exertion.

"Spare him! spare him!" cried the boy, leaping forwards. "I am the prey you seek!"

"Well met, my young Lord," was the stern reply. "You have found yourself a worthy way of life, and an honourable companion."

"Honourable indeed, if faithfulness be honour!" replied the boy. "Myself I yield, Sir; but spare him, if yet he lives!—O Adam, my only friend!" he sobbed, as kneeling over him, he raised his head, undid his collar, and parted the black locks, to seek for the mark of the blow, whence blood was fast oozing.

"He lives—he will do well enough," said the hunter. "Now, tell me, boy— what brought you here?"

"The loving fidelity of this man!" was the prompt reply:- "a Poitevin, a falconer at Kenilworth, who found me sore wounded on the field at Evesham, and ever since has tended me as never vassal tended lord; and now—now hath he indeed died for me!" and the boy, endeavouring to raise the inanimate form, dropped heavy tears on the senseless face.

"True," rigidly spoke the hunter, though there was somewhat of a quivering of the muscles of the cheek discernible amid the curls of his chestnut beard: "robbery is not the wonted service demanded of retainers."

"Poor Adam!" said the youth with a flash of spirit, "at least he never stripped the peaceful homestead and humble farmer, like the royal purveyors!"

"Ha—young rebel!" exclaimed the hunter. "Know you what you say?"

"I reck not," replied the boy: "you have slain my father and my brothers, and now you have slain my last and only friend. Do as you will with me—only for my mother's sake, let it not be a shameful death; and let my sister Eleanor have my poor Leonillo. And let me, too, leave this gold with the priest of Alton, that my true-hearted loving Adam may have fit burial and masses."

"I tell thee, boy, he is in no more need of a burial than thou or I. I touched him warily. Here—his face more to the air."

And the stranger bent down, and with his powerful strength lifted the heavy form of Adam, so that the boy could better support him. Then taking some wine from the hunting-flask slung to his own shoulder, he applied some drops to the bruise. The smart produced signs of life, and the hunter put his flask into the boy's hand, saying, "Give him a draught, and then—" he put his finger to his own lips, and stood somewhat apart.

Adam opened his eyes, and made some inarticulate murmurs; then, the liquor being held to his lips, he drank, and with fresh vigour raised himself.

"The boy!—where is he? What has chanced? Is it you, Sir? Where is the rogue? Fled, the villain? We shall have the Prince upon us next! I must after him, and cut his story short! Your hand, Sir!"

"Nay, Adam—your hurt!"

"A broken head! Tush, 'tis naught! Here, your hand! Canst not lend a hand to help a man up in your own service?" he added testily, as stiff and dizzy he sat up and tried to rise. "You might have sent an arrow to stop his traitorous tongue; but there is no help in you!" he added, provoked at seeing a certain embarrassment about the youth. "Desert me at this pinch! It is not like his father's son!" and he was sinking back, when at sight of the hunter he stumbled eagerly to his feet, but only to stagger against a tree.

"You are my prisoner!" said the calm deep voice.

"Well and good," said Adam surlily. "But let the lad go free: he is a yeoman's son, who came but to bear me company."

"And learn thy trade? Goodly lessons in falling unawares on the King's huntsmen, and sending arrows after them! Fair breeding, in sooth!" repeated the stranger, standing with his arms crossed upon his mighty breadth of chest, and looking at Adam with a still, grave, commanding blue eye, that seemed to pierce him and hold him down, as it were, and a countenance whose youthfulness and perfect regularity of feature did but enhance its exceeding severity of expression. "You know the meed of robbery and murder?"

"A halter and a bough," said Adam readily. "Well and good; but I tell thee that concerns not the boy—since," he added bitterly, "he is too meek and tender so much as to lift a hand in his own cause! He has never crossed the laws."

"I understand you, friend," said the hunter: "he is a valued charge- -maybe the son of one of the traitor barons. Take my advice—yield him to the King's justice, and secure your own pardon."

"Out, miscreant!" shouted Adam; and was about to spring at him again, but the powerful arm collared him, and he recognized at once that he was like a child in that grasp. He ground his teeth with rage and muttered, "That a fellow with such thews should give such dastardly counsel, and HE yonder not lift a finger to aid!"

"Wilt follow me," composedly demanded the stranger, "with hands free? or must I bind them?"

"Follow?" replied Adam, ruefully looking at the boy with eyes full of reproach—"ay, follow to any gallows thou wilt—and the nearest tree were the best! Come on!"

"I have no warrant," returned the grave hunter.

"Tush! what warrant is needed for hanging a well-known outlaw—made so by the Prince's tender mercies? The Prince will thank thee, man, for ridding the realm of the robber who fell on the treasurer bearing the bags from Leicester!"

And meanwhile, with uncouth cunning, Adam was striving to telegraph by winks and gestures to the boy who had so grievously disappointed him, that the moment of his own summary execution would be an excellent one for his companion's escape.

But the eye, so steady yet so quick under its somewhat drooping eyelid, detected the simple stratagem.

"I trow the Prince might thank me more for bringing in this charge of thine."

"Small thanks, I trow, for laying hands on a poor orphan—the son of a Poitevin man-at-arms—that I kept with me for love of his father, though he is fitter for a convent than the green wood!" added Adam, with the same sound of keen reproach and disappointment in his voice.

"That shall we learn at Guildford," replied the stranger. "There are means of teaching a man to speak."

"None that will serve with me," stoutly responded Adam.

"That shall we see," was the brief answer.

And he signed to his prisoners to move on before him, taking care so to interpose his stately person between them, that there should be no communication by word, far less by look.

CHAPTER II—THE LADY OF THE FOREST

"Behold how mercy softeneth still
  The haughtiest heart that beats:
Pride with disdain may he answered again,
  But pardon at once defeats!"—S. M.

The so-called forest was in many parts mere open heath, thickly adorned by the beautiful purple ling, blending into a rich carpet with the dwarf furze, and backed by thickets of trees in the hollows of the ground.

Across this wild country the tall forester conducted his captives in silence— moving along with a pace that evidently cost him so little exertion, and was so steady and even, that his companions might have supposed it slow, had they only watched it, and not been obliged to keep up with it. Light of foot as the youth was, he was at times reduced to an almost breathless run; and Adam plodded along, with strides that worked his arms and shoulders in sympathy.

After about three miles, when the boy was beginning to feel as if he must soon be in danger of lagging, they came into a dip of the ground where stood a long, low, irregular building, partly wood and partly stone, roofed with shingle in some parts, in others with heather. The last addition, a deep porch, still retained the fresh tints of the bark on the timber sides, and the purple of the ling that roofed it.

Sheds and out-houses surrounded it; dogs in couples, horses, grooms, and foresters, were congregated in the background; but around this new porch were gathered a troop of peasant women, children, and aged men. The fine bald brow and profile of the old peasant, the eager face of the curly-haired child, the worn countenance of the hard- tasked mother, were all uplifted towards the doorway, in which stood, slightly above them, a lady, with two long plaited flaxen tresses descending on her shoulders, under a black silken veil, that disclosed a youthful countenance, full of pure calm loveliness, of a simple but dignified and devotional expression, that might have befitted an angel of charity. A priest and a lady were dispensing loaves and warm garments to the throng around; but each gift was accompanied by a gentle word from the lady, framed with difficulty to their homely English tongue, but listened to even by uncomprehending ears like a strain of Church music.

Adam had expected the forester to turn aside to the group of servants, but in blank amazement saw him lead the way through the poor at the gate; and advancing to the porch with a courteous bending of his head, he said in the soft Provencal—far more familiar than English to Adam's ears—"Hast room for another suppliant, mi Dona?"

The sweet fair face lighted up with a sudden sunbeam of joy; and a musical voice replied. "Welcome, my dearest Lord: much did I need thee to hear the plaints of some of these thy lieges, which my ears can scarce understand! But why art thou alone? or rather, why thus strangely accompanied?"

"These are the captives won by my single arm, whom, according to all laws of chivalry, thine own true knight thus lays at thy feet, fair lady mine, to be disposed of at thine own gracious will and pleasure."

And a smile of such sweetness lightened his features, that a murmur of "Blessings on his comely face!" ran through the assembly; and Adam indulged in a gruff startled murmur of "'Tis the Prince, or the devil himself!" while his young master, comprehending the gesture of the Prince, and overborne by the lovely winning graces of the Princess, stepped forward, doffing his cap and bending his knee, and signing to Adam to follow his example.

"Thou hast been daring peril again!" said the Princess, holding her husband's arm, and looking up into his face with lovingly reproachful yet exulting eyes. "Yet I will not be troubled! Naught is danger to thee! And yet alone and unarmed to encounter such a sturdy savage as I see yonder! But there is blood on his brow! Let his hurt be looked to ere we speak of his fate."

"He is at thy disposal, mi Dona," returned Edward: "thou art the judge of both, and shall decide their lot when thou hast heard their tale."

"It can scarce be a very dark one," replied Eleanor, "or thou wouldst never have led them to such a judge!" Then turning to the prisoners, she began to say in her foreign English, "Follow the good father, friends—" when she broke off at fuller sight of the boy's countenance, and exclaimed in Provencal, "I know the like of that face and mien!"

"Truly dost thou know it," her husband replied; "but peace till thou hast cleared thy present court, and we can be private.—Follow the priest," he added, "and await the Princess's pleasure."

They obeyed; and the priest led them through a side-door, through which they could still hear Eleanor's sweet Castillian voice laying before her husband her difficulties in comprehending her various petitioners. The priest being English, was hardly more easily understood than his flock; and her lady spoke little but langue d'oui, the Northern French, which was as little serviceable in dealing with her Spanish and Provencal as with the rude West-Saxon-English. Edward's deep manly tones were to be heard, however, now interrogating the peasants in their own tongue, now briefly interpreting to his wife in Provencal; and a listener could easily gather that his hand was as bounteous, his heart as merciful, as hers, save where attacks on the royal game had been requited by the trouble complained of; and that in such cases she pleaded in vain.

11

The captives, whom her husband had surrendered to her mercy, had been led into a great, long, low hall, with rudely-timbered sides, and rough beams to the roof, with a stone floor, and great open fire, over which a man-cook was chattering French to his bewildered English scullion. An oak table, and settles on either side of it, ran the whole length of the hall; and here the priest bade the two prisoners seat themselves. They obeyed—the boy slouching his cap over his face, averting it, and keeping as far as possible from the group of servants near the fire. The priest called for bread, meat, and beer, to be set before them; and after a moment's examination of Adam's bruise, applied the simple remedy that was all it required, and left them to their meal. Adam took this opportunity to growl in an undertone, "Does HE there know you?" The reply was a nod of assent. "And you knew him?" Another nod; and then the boy, looking heedfully round, added in a quick, undertone, "Not till you were down. Then he helped me to restore you. You forgive me, Adam, now?" and he held out his hand, and wrung the rugged one of the forester.

"What should I forgive! Poor lad! you could not have striven in the Longshanks' grasp! I was a fool not to guess how it was, when I saw you not knowing which way to look!"

"Hush!" broke in the youth with uplifted hand, as a page of about his own age came daintily into the hall, gathering his green robe about him as if he disdained the neighbourhood, and holding his head high under his jaunty tall feathered cap.

"Outlaws!" he said, speaking English, but with a strong foreign accent, and as if it were a great condescension, "the gracious Princess summons you to her presence. Follow me!"

The colour rushed to the boy's temples, and a retort was on his lips, but he struggled to withhold it; and likewise speaking English, said, "I would we could have some water, and make ourselves meeter for her presence."

"Scarce worth the pains," returned the page. "As if thou couldst ever be meet for her presence! She had rather be rid of thee promptly, than wait to be regaled with thy May-day braveries—honest lad!"

Again the answer was only restrained with exceeding difficulty; and there was a scornful smile on the young prisoner's cheek, that caused the page to exclaim angrily, "What means that insolence, malapert boy?"

But there was no time for further strife; for the door was pushed open, and the Prince's voice called, "Hamlyn de Valence, why tarry the prisoners?"

"Only, Sir," returned Hamlyn, "that this young robber is offended that he hath not time to deck himself out in his last stolen gold chain, to gratify the

Princess!"

"Peace, Hamlyn," returned the Prince: "thou speakest thou knowest not what. —Come hither, boy," he added, laying his hand on his young captive's shoulder, and putting him through the door with a familiarity that astonished Hamlyn—all the more, when he found that while both prisoners were admitted, he himself was excluded!

Princess Eleanor was alone in another chamber of the sylvan lodge, hung with tapestry representing hunting scenes, the floor laid with deer-skins, and deer's antlers projecting from the wall, to support the feminine properties that marked it as her special abode. She was standing when they entered; and was turning eagerly with outstretched hand and face of recognition, when Prince Edward checked her by saying, "Nay, the cause is not yet tried:" and placing her in a large carved oaken chair, where she sat with a lily-like grace and dignity, half wondering, but following his lead, he proceeded, "Sit thou there, fair dame, and exercise thy right, as judge of the two captives whom I place at thy feet."

"And you, my Lord?" she asked.

"I stand as their accuser," said Edward. "Advance, prisoners!—Now, most fair judge, what dost thou decree for the doom of Adam de Gourdon, rebel first, and since that the terror of our royal father's lieges, the robber of his treasurers, the rifler of our Cousin Pembroke's jewellery, the slayer of our deer?"

"Alas! my Lord, why put such questions to me," said Eleanor imploringly, "unless, as I would fain hope, thou dost but jest?"

"Do I speak jest, Gourdon?" said Edward, regarding Adam with a lion- like glance.

"'Tis all true," growled Adam.

"And," proceeded the Prince, "if thy gentle lips refuse to utter the doom merited by such deeds, what wilt thou say to hear that, not content with these traitorous deeds of his own, he fosters the treason of others? Here stands a young rebel, who would have perished at Evesham, but for the care and protection of this Gourdon- -who healed his wounds, guarded him, robbed for him, for him spurned the offer of amnesty, and finally, set on thine own husband in Alton Wood—all to shelter yonder young traitor from the hands of justice! Speak the sentence he merits, most just of judges!"

"The sentence he merits?" said Eleanor, with swimming eyes. "Oh! would that I were indeed monarch, to dispense life or death! What he merits he shall have, from my whole heart—mine own poor esteem for his fidelity, and our

13

joint entreaties to the King for his pardon! Brave man—thou shalt come with me to seek thy pardon from King Henry!"

"Thanks, Lady," said Adam with rude courtesy; "but it were better to seek my young lord's."

"My own dear young cousin!" exclaimed Eleanor, laying aside her assumed judicial power, and again holding out her hands to him, "we deemed you slain!"

"Yes, come hither," said Edward, "my jailer at Hereford—the rebel who drew his maiden sword against his King and uncle—the outlaw who would try whether Leicester fits as well as Huntingdon with a bandit life! What hast thou to say for thyself, Richard de Montfort?"

"That my fate, be it what it may, must not stand in the way of Adam's pardon!" said Richard, standing still, without response to the Princess's invitation. "My Lord, you have spoken much of his noble devotion to me for my father's sake; but you know not the half of what he has done and dared for me. Oh! plead for him, Lady!"

"Plead for him!" said Eleanor: "that will I do with all my heart; and well do I know that the good old King will weep with gratitude to him for having preserved the life of his young nephew. Yes, Richard, oft have we grieved for thee, my husband's kind young companion in his captivity, and mourned that no tidings could be gained of thee!"

It was not Richard who replied to this winning address. He stood flushed, irresolute, with eyes resolutely cast down, as if to avoid seeing the Princess's sweet face.

Adam, however, spoke: "Then, Lady, I am indeed beholden to you; provided that the boy is safe."

"He is safe," said Prince Edward. "His age is protection sufficient.—My young cousin, thou art no outlaw: thine uncle will welcome thee gladly; and a career is open to thee where thou mayst redeem the honour of thy name."

The colour came with deeper crimson to the boy's cheek, as he answered in a choked voice, "My father's name needs no redemption!"

Simultaneously a pleading interjection from the Princess, and a warning growl from De Gourdon, admonished Richard that he was on perilous ground; but the Prince responded in a tone of deep feeling, "Well said, Richard: the term does not befit that worthy name. I should have said that I would fain help thee to maintain its honour. My page once, wilt thou be so again? and one day my knight—my trusty baron?"

"How can I?" said Richard, still in the same undertone, subdued but determined: "it was you who slew him and my brothers!"

"Nay, nay!" exclaimed the Princess: "the poor boy thinks all his kindred are slain!"

"And they are not!" cried Richard, raising his face with sudden animation. "They are safe?"

"Thy brother Henry died with—with the Earl," said Eleanor; "but all the rest are safe, and in France."

"And my mother and sister?" asked Richard.

"They are likewise abroad," said the Prince. "And, Richard, thou art free to join them if thou wilt. But listen first to me. We tarry yet two days at this forest lodge: remain with us for that space— thy name and rank unknown if thou wilt—and if thou shalt still look on me as guilty of thy father's death, and not as a loving kinsman, who honoured him deeply, I will send thee safely to the coast, with letters to my uncle, the King of France."

Richard raised his head with a searching glance, to see whether this were invitation or command.

"Thou art my captive," said Eleanor softly, coming towards him with a young matron's caressing manner to a boy whom she would win and encourage.

"Not captive, but guest," said Edward; but Richard perceived in the tones that no choice was left him, as far as these two days were concerned.

CHAPTER III—ALTON LODGE

"Ever were his sons hawtayn,
And bold for their vilanye;
Bothe to knight and sweyn
Did they vilanye."
Old Ballad of Simon de Montforte.

For the first time for many a month, Richard de Montfort lay down to sleep in a pallet bed, instead of a couch of heather; but his heart was ill at ease. He was the fourth son of the great Earl of Leicester, Simon de Montfort; and for the earlier years of his life, he had been under the careful training of the excellent chaplain, Adam de Marisco, a pupil and disciple of the great Robert Grostete, Bishop of Lincoln. His elder brothers had early left this wholesome control; pushed forward by the sad circumstances that finally drove their father to take up arms against the King, and strangers to the noble temper that actuated him in his championship of the English people, they became mere lawless rebels—fiercely profiting by his elevation, not for the good of the people, but for their own gratification.

Richard had been still a mere boy under constant control, and being intelligent, spirited, and docile, had been an especial favourite with his father. To him the great Earl had been the model of all that was admirable, wise, and noble; deeply religious, just, and charitable, and perfect in all the arts of chivalry and accomplishments of peace—a tender and indulgent father, and a firm and wise head of a household—he had been ardently loved and looked up to by the young son, who had perhaps more in common with him by nature than any other of the family.

Wrongs and injuries had been heaped upon Montfort by the weak and fickle King, who would far better have understood him, if, like the selfish kinsmen who encircled the throne, he had struggled for his own advantage, and not for the maintenance of the Great Charter. Richard was too young to remember the early days when his elder brothers had been companions, almost on equal terms, to their first cousins, the King's sons; his whole impression of his parents' relations with the court was of injustice and perfidy from the King and his counsellors, vehemently blamed by his mother and brothers, but sometimes palliated by his father, who almost always, even at the worst, pleaded the King's helplessness, and Prince Edward's honourable intentions. Understanding little of the rights of the case, Richard only saw his father as the maintainer of the laws, and defender of the oppressed against covenant breakers; and when the appeal to arms was at length made, he saw the white cross assumed by his father and brothers, in full belief that the war in defence of Magna Carta was indeed as sacred as a crusade, and he had earnestly entreated to be allowed to bear arms; but he had been deemed as yet too young, and thus had had no share in the victory of Lewes, save the full triumph in it that was felt by all at Kenilworth. Afterwards, when sent to be Prince Edward's page at Hereford, he was prepared to regard his royal cousin as a ferocious enemy, and was much taken by surprise to find him a graceful courtly knight, peculiarly gentle in manner, loving music, romances, and all chivalrous accomplishments; and far from the pride and haughtiness that had been the theme of all the vassals who assembled at Kenilworth, he was gracious to all, and distinguished his young page by treating him as a kinsman and favourite companion; showing him indeed far more consideration than ever he had received from his unruly turbulent brothers.

When Edward had effected his escape, and had joined the Mortimers and Clares, Richard had gone home, where his expressions of affection for the

Prince were listened to by his father, indeed, with a well- pleased though melancholy smile, and an augury that one day his brave godson would shake off the old King's evil counsellors, and show himself in his true and noble colouring. His brothers, however, laughed and chid any word about the Prince's kindness. Edward's flattery and seduction, they declared, had won the young De Clare from their cause. And in vain did their father assure them that they had lost the alliance of the house of Gloucester solely by their own over-bearing injustice—a tyranny worse than had been exercised under the name of the King.

With Henry of Winchester in their hands, however, theirs seemed the loyal cause; and Richard had, by the influence of his elders, been made ashamed of his regard for the Prince, and looked upon it as a treacherous rebellion, when Edward mustered his forces, and fell upon Leicester and his followers. His father had mournfully yielded to the boy's entreaty to remain with him, instead of being sent away with his mother and the younger ones for security: an honourable death, said the Earl, might be better for him than an outlawed and proscribed life. And thus Richard had heard his father's exclamation on marking the well-ordered advance of the Royalists: "They have learnt this style from me. Now, God have mercy on our souls, for our bodies are the Prince's!"

And when Henry, his eldest son, spoke words of confidence, entreating him not to despair, he had answered, "I do not, my son; but your presumption, and the pride of thy brothers, have brought me to this pass. I firmly believe I shall die for the cause of God and justice."

Richard had shared his father's last Communion, received his last blessing, and had stood beside him in the desperate ring, which in true English fashion died on the field of battle, but never was driven from it. Since that time, the boy's life had been a wandering amid outlaws and peasants—all in one mind of bitter hatred to the court for its cruel vexations and oppressions, and of intense love and regret for their champion, Sir Simon the Righteous, of whose beneficence tales were everywhere told, rising at every step into greater wonder, until at length they were enhanced into miracles, wrought by his severed head and hands. Each day had made the boy prouder of his father's memory, more deeply incensed against the Court party that had brought about his fall; and keen and bitter were his feelings at finding himself in the hands of the Prince himself. He chafed all the more at feeling the ascendency which Edward's lofty demeanour and personal kindness had formerly exerted over him, reviving again by force of habit; he hated himself for not having at once challenged his father's murderer; so as, if he could not do more, to have died by his hand; and he despised himself the more, for knowing that all he could have said would have been good-naturedly put down by the Prince; all he could have done would have been but like a gnat's efforts against that mighty strength. Then how despicable it was to be sensible, in spite of himself, that this atmosphere of courtly refinement was far more natural to him—the son of a Provencal noble, and of a princess mother—than the rude forest life he had lately led. The greenwood liberty had its charms; and he had truly loved Adam de Gourdon; but the soft tones and refined accents were like a note of home to him; and though he had never seen the Princess before—she having been sent to the Court of St. Louis during the troubles—yet the whole of the interview gave him an inexplicable sense of being again among kindred and friends. He told himself that it was base, resolved that he would show himself determined to cast in his lot with his exiled brethren, and made up his mind to maintain a dignified silence during these two days, and at the end of them to leave with the Prince a challenge, to be fought out when he should have attained manly strength and skill in arms.

In pursuance of this resolution, he appeared at the morning mass and meal still grave and silent, and especially avoiding young Hamlyn de Valence, who, as the son of one of the half brothers of Henry III., stood in the same relationship to Prince Edward and to Richard, whose mother was the sister of King Henry. Probably Hamlyn had had a hint from the Prince, for though he regarded young Montfort with no friendly eyes, he yielded him an equality of precedence, which hardly consorted with Richard's rude forest garments.

The chase was the order of the day. The Prince rode forth with a boar spear to hunt one of these monsters of the wood, of which vague reports had reached him, unconfirmed, till Adam de Gourdon had undertaken to show him the creature's lair. He had proposed to Richard to join the hunt; but the boy, firm to his resolution of accepting no favour from him, that could be helped, had refused as curtly as he could; and then, not without a feeling of disappointment, had stood holding Leonillo in, as the gallant train of hunters rode down the woodland glade, and he figured to himself the brave sport in which they would soon be engaged.

The most part of the day was spent by him in lying under a tree, with his dog by his side, thinking over the scenes of his earlier life, which had passed by his childish mind like those of a drama, in which he had no part nor comprehension, but which now, with clearer perceptions, he strove to recall and explain to himself. Ever his father's stately figure was the centre of his recollections, whether receiving tidings of infractions of engagements, taking prompt measures for action, or striving to repress the violence of his sons and partizans, or it might be gazing on his younger boys with sad anxiety. Richard well remembered his saying, when he heard that his sons, Simon and Guy, had been plundering the merchant ships in the Channel: "Alas! alas! when I was more loyal to the law than to the Crown, I little deemed that I was rearing a brood who would scorn all law and loyalty!"

And well too did Richard recollect that when the proposal had been made that he should become the attendant of the Prince at Hereford, his father had told him that here he would see the mirror of all that was knightly and virtuous; and had added, on the loud outcry of the more prejudiced brothers: "It is only the truth. Were it not that the King's folly and his perjured counsellors had come between my nephew Edward and his better self, we should have in him a sovereign who might fitly be reckoned as a tenth worthy. It is his very duty to a misruled father that has ranged him against us."

"Yet," thought Richard, "on the man who thus thought and spoke of him the Prince could make savage warfare; nay, offer his senseless corpse foul despite. How can I tarry these two days in such keeping? I had rather—if he will still keep me—be a captive in his lowest dungeon, than eat of his bread as a guest! By our Lady, I will tell him so to his face! I will none of his favours! Alone I will go to the coast- -alone make my way to Simon and Guy, with no letters to the French king! All kings, however saintly they may be called, are in league, and make common cause; as said my poor brother Henry, when the Mise of Lewes was to be laid before this Frenchman! I will none of them! Pshaw! is this the Princess coming? I trust she will not see me. I want none of her fair words."

He had prepared himself to be ungracious; but his courtly breeding was too much of an instinct with him for him not to rise, doff his cap, and stand aside, as Eleanor of Castille slowly moved towards the woodland path, with her graceful Spanish step, followed, but at some distance, by two of her women. She turned as she was passing him, and smiled with a sweet radiance that would have won him instantly, had he not heard his elder brothers sneer at the cheap coin of royal smiles. He only bowed; but Leonillo was more accessible, and started forward to pay his homage of dignified blandishments to the queenly sweetness that pleased his canine appreciation. Richard was forced to step forth, call him in, and make his excuses; but the Princess responded by praises of the noble animal, and caresses, to which Leonillo replied with a grand gratitude, that showed him as nobly bred as his young master.

"Thou art a gallant creature," said Eleanor, her hand upon the proud head; "and no doubt as faithful as beautiful!"

"Faithful to the death, Lady," replied Richard warmly.

"He is thine own, I trow," said the Princess,—"not thy groom's? I remember, that when thy brave father brought my lord and me back from our bridal at

Burgos, he procured two hounds in the Pyrenees, of meseems, such a breed."

"True, Lady; they were the parents of my Leonillo," said Richard, gratified, in spite of himself.

"How well I remember," continued Eleanor, "that first sight of the great Earl. My brothers had teased me for going so far north, and told me the English were mere rude islanders—boorish, and unlettered; but, child as I was, scarce eleven years old, I could perceive the nobleness of the Earl. 'If all thy new subjects be like him,' said my brother to me, 'thou wilt reign over a race of kings.' And how good he was to me when I wept at leaving my home and friends! How he framed his tongue to speak my own Castillian to me; how he comforted me, when the Queen, my mother-in-law, required more dignity of me than I yet knew how to assume; and how he chid my boy bridegroom for showing scant regard for his girl bride!" said Eleanor, smiling at the recollection, as the beloved wife of eleven years could well afford to do. "I mind me well that he found me weeping, because my Edward had tied the scarf I gave him on the neck of one of those very dogs, and the fatherly counsel he gave me. Ah, Leonillo, thy wise wistful face brings back many thoughts to my mind! I am glad I may honour thee for fidelity!"

"Indeed you may, Lady," said Richard. "It was he that above all saved my life."

"Prithee let me hear," said the Princess, who had already so moved on, while herself speaking, as to draw Richard into walking with her along the path that had been cleared under the beech trees. "We have so much longed to know thy fate."

"I cannot tell you much, Lady," returned Richard. "The last thing I recollect on that dreadful day was, that my father asked for quarter- -for us—for my brother Henry and me. We heard the reply: 'No quarter for traitors!' and Henry fell before us a dead man. My father shouted, 'By the arm of St. James, it is time for me to die!' I saw him, with his sword in both hands, cut down a wild Welshman who was rushing on me. Then I saw no more, till in the moonlight I was awakened by this dog's cool tongue licking the blood from my face, and heard his low whining over me."

"Good dog, good dog!" murmured Eleanor, caressing the animal. "And thou, Richard, thou wert sorely wounded?"

"Sorely," said Richard; "my side had been pierced with a lance, a Welsh two-handed sword had broken through my helmet, and well-nigh cleft my skull; and the men-at-arms, riding over me I suppose, must have broken my leg, for I could not move: and oh! I felt it hard that I had yet to die. Then, Lady, came lights and murmuring voices. They were Mortimer's plundering Welsh robbers. I heard their wild gibbering tongue; and I knew how it would be with me, should they see the white cross on my breast. But, Lady, Leonillo stood over me. His lion bark chased them aside; and when one bolder than the rest came near the mound where we lay, good Leonillo flew at his savage throat. I heard the struggle as I lay—the growls of the dog, the howls of the man; and then they were cut short. And next I heard de Gourdon's gruff voice commending the good hound, whose note had led him to the spot, from the woods, where he was hiding after the battle. The faithful beast sprang from him, and in a moment more had led him to me. Then—ah, then, Lady! when Adam had freed me from my broken helm, and lifted me in his arms, what a sight had I! Oh, what a field that harvest moon shone upon! how thickly heaped was that little mound! And there was my father's face up-turned in the white moonlight! O Lady, never in hall or bower could it have been so peaceful, or so majestic! I bade Adam lay me down by his side, and keep guard through the night with Leonillo; but he said that the plunderers would come in numbers too great for him, and that he must care for the living rather than the dead; and withstand him as I would, he bore me away. O Lady, Lady, foul wrong was done when we were gone!"

"Think not on that," said Eleanor; "it bitterly grieved my lord that so it should have been. Thou knowest, I hope, that he was the chief mourner when those honoured limbs were laid in the holy ground at Evesham Abbey. They told me, who saw him that day, that his weeping for his godfather and his Cousin Henry overcame all joy in his victory. And I can assure thee, dear Richard, that when, three months after, I came to him at Canterbury, just after he had been with thy mother at Dover, even then he was sad and mournful. He said that the wisest and best baron in England had been made a rebel of, and then slain; and he was full of sorrow for thee, only then understanding from thy mother that thou hadst been in the battle at all, and that nothing had been heard of thee. He said thou wert the most like to thy father of all his sons; and truly I knew thee at once by thine eyes, Richard. Where wast thou all these months?"

"At first," said Richard, "I was in an anchoret's cell, in the wall of a church. So please you, Madame, I must not name names; but when Adam, bearing me faint and well-nigh dying on his back, saw the twinkling light in the churchyard, he knocked, and entreated aid. The good anchoret pitied my need at first, and when he learnt my name, he gave me shelter for my father's sake, the friend of all religious men. I lay on his little bed, in the chamber in the wall, till I could again walk. Meanwhile, Adam watched in the woods at hand, and from time to time came at night to see how I fared, and bring me tidings. Simon was still holding out Kenilworth, and we hoped to join him there; but when we set forth I was still lame, and too feeble to go far in a day; and we fell in with—within short, with a band of robbers, who detained us, half as guests, half as captives. They needed Adam's stout arm; and there was a shrewd, gray, tough old fellow, who had been in Robin Hood's band, and was looked up to as a sort of prince among them, who was bent on making us one with them. Lady, you would smile to hear how the old man used to sit by me as I lay on the rushes, and talk of outlawry, as Father Adam de Marisco used to talk of learning—as a good and noble science, decaying for want of spirit and valour in these days. It was all laziness, he said; barons and princes must needs have their wars, and use up all the stout men that were fit to bend a bow in a thicket. If the Prince went on at this rate, he said, there would soon be not an honest outlaw to be found in England! But he was a kind old man, and very good to me; and he taught me how to shoot with the long bow better than ever our master at Odiham could. However, I could not brook the spoiler's life, and the band did not trust me; so, as we found that Kenilworth had fallen, as soon as my strength had returned to me, we stole away from the outlaws, and came southwards, hoping to find my mother at Odiham. Hearing that Odiham too was gone from us, we have lurked in Alton Wood till means should serve us for reaching the coast."

"Till thou hast found the friend who has longed for thee, and sought for thee," replied Eleanor. "What didst thou do, young Richard, to win my husband's heart so entirely in his captivity?"

"I know not, Lady, why he should take thought for me," bluntly said Richard, with a return of the sensation of being coaxed and talked over.

"Methinks I can tell thee one cause," returned the Princess. "Was there not a time when thou didst overhear him concerting with Thomas de Clare the plan of an escape, and thou didst warn them that thou wast at hand; ay, and yet didst send notice to thy father?"

"Yes," answered Richard with surprise; "I could do no other."

"Even so," said Eleanor. "And thus didst thou win the esteem of thy kinsman. 'The stripling is loyal and trustworthy,' he has said to me; 'pity that such a heart should be pierced in an inglorious field. Would that I could find him, and strive to return to him something of what his father's care hath wrought for me.' Richard, trust me, it would be a real joy and lightening of his grief to have thee with him."

"Grief, Madame!" repeated Richard. "I little thought he grieved for my father, who, but for him, would be—" and a sob checked him, as the contrast rose before him of the great Earl and beautiful Countess presiding over their large family and princely household, and the scattered ruined state of all at present.

"He shall answer that question himself," said Eleanor. "See, here he comes to meet us by the beechwood alley."

And in fact, a form, well suited to its setting within the stately aisles of the beech trees, was pacing towards them. The chase had ended, and hearing that his wife had walked forth into the wood, the Prince had come by another path to meet her, and his rare and beautiful smile shone out as he saw who was her companion. "Art making friends with my young cousin?" he said affectionately.

"I would fain do so," replied Eleanor; "but alas, my Lord! he feels that there is a long dark reckoning behind, that stands in the way of our friendship."

Richard looked down, and did not speak. The Princess had put his thought into words.

"Richard," said the Prince, "I feel the same. It is for that very cause that I seek to have thee with me. Hear me. Thou art grown older, and hast seen man's work and man's sorrows, since I left thee on the hill-side at Hereford. Thou canst see, perchance, that a question hath two sides—though it is not given to all men to do so. Hearken then.—Thy father was the greatest man I have known—nay, but for the thought of my uncle of France, I should say the holiest. He was my teacher in all knightly doings, and in all kingly thoughts, such as I pray may be with me through life. It was from him I learnt that this royal, this noble power, is not given to exalt ourselves, but as a trust for the welfare of others. It was the spring of action that was with him through life."

"It was," murmured Richard, calling to mind many a saying of his father's.

"And fain would he have impressed it on all around," added Edward: "but there were others who deemed that kingly power was but a means of enjoyment, and that restraint was an outrage on the crown. They drew one way, the Earl drew the other, and, as his noble nature prompted him, made common cause with the injured. It skills not to go through the past. Those whom he joined had selfish aims, and pushed him on; and as the crown had been led to invade the rights of the vassals, so the vassals invaded my father's rights. Oaths were extorted, though both sides knew they could never be observed; and between violences, now on one side, now on the other, the right course could scarce be kept. The Earl imagined that, with my father in his hands, removed from all other influences, he could give England the happy days they talk of her having enjoyed under my patron St. Edward; but, as thou knowest, Richard, the authority he held, being unlawful, was unregarded, and its worst transgressors came out of his own bosom. He could not enforce the terms on which I had yielded myself—he could not even prevent my father from being a mere captive; and for the English folk, their miseries were but multiplied by the tyrants who had arisen."

"It was no doing of his," said Richard, with cheek hotly glowing.

"None know that better than I," said the Prince; "but if he had snatched the bridle from a feeble hand, it was only to find that the steed could not be ruled by him. What was left for me but to break my bonds, and deliver my father, in the hope that, being come to man's estate, I might set matters on a surer footing? I had hoped—I had greatly hoped, so to rule affairs, that the Earl might own that his training had not been lost on his nephew, and that the Crown might be trusted not to infringe the Charter. I had hoped that he might yet be my wisest counsellor. But, Richard, I too had supporters who outran my commands. Bitter hatred and malice had been awakened, and cruel resolves that none should be spared. When I returned from bearing my father, bleeding and dismayed, from the battle, whither he had been cruelly led, it was to find that my orders had been disobeyed—that there had been foul and cruel slaughter; and that all my hopes that my uncle of Leicester would forgive me and look friendly on me were ended!"

The Prince's lip trembled as he spoke, and tears glistened in his eyes; and the evident struggle to repress his feelings, brought home deeply and forcibly the conviction to Richard that his sorrow was genuine.

He could not speak for some seconds; then he added: "I marvel not that I am looked on among you as guilty of his blood. Simon and Guy regard me as one with whom they are at deadly feud, and cannot understand that it was their own excesses that armed those merciless hands against him. Even my aunt shrank from me, and implored my mercy as though I were a ruthless tyrant. But thou, Richard, thou hast inherited enough of thy father's mind to be able to understand how unwillingly was my share in his fall, and how great would be my comfort and joy in being good kinsman to one of his sons."

The strong man's generous pleading was most touching. Richard bowed his head; the Princess watched him eagerly. The boy spoke at last in perplexity. "My Lord, you know better than I. Would it be knightly, would it be honourable?"

The Princess started in some indignation at such a question to her husband; but Edward understood the boy better, and said, "That which is most Christian is most knightly." Then pausing: "Ask thine heart, Richard; which would thy father choose for thee—to live in such guidance as I hope will ever be found in my household, or to share the wandering, I fear me freebooting, life of thy brothers?"

Richard could not forget how his father had sternly withheld him from going with Simon to besiege Pevensey. He knew that these two brethren had long been a pain and grief to his father; and began to understand that the nephew, with whom the Earl's last battle had been fought, was nevertheless his truest pupil.

"Thou wilt remain," said Edward decisively; "and let us strive one day to bring to pass the state of things for which thy father and I fought alike, though, alas! in opposite ranks."

"If my mother consents," said Richard, his head bent down, and uttering the words with the more difficulty, because he felt so strongly drawn towards his cousin, who never seemed so mighty as in his condescension.

"Then, Richard de Montfort," said Edward gravely, "let us render to one another the kiss of peace, as kinsmen who have put away all thought of wrong between them."

Richard looked up; and the Prince bending his lofty head, there was exchanged between them that solemn embrace, which in the early middle ages was the deepest token of amity.

And with that kiss, it was as though the soul of Richard de Montfort were knit to the soul of Edward of England with the heart-whole devotion, composed of affection and loyal homage to a great character, which ever since the days of the bond between the son of the doomed King of Israel and the youthful slayer of the Philistine champion, has been one of the noblest passions of a young heart.

CHAPTER IV—THE TRANSLATION

"Now in gems their relics lie,
And their names in blazonry,
And their forms in storied panes
Gleam athwart their own loved fanes."
Lyra Innocentium.

If novelty has its charms, so has old age, and to us the great abbey church of Westminster has become doubly beloved by long generations of affection, and doubly beautiful by the softening handiwork of time and of smoke.

Yet what a glorious sight must it not have been when it was fresh from the hands of the builder, the creamy stone clear and sharp at every angle, and each moulding and flower true and perfect as the chisel had newly left it. The deep archway of the west front opened in stately magnificence, and yet with a light loftiness hitherto unknown in England, and somewhat approaching to the style in which the great French cathedrals were then rising. And its accompaniments were, on the one hand the palace and hall, on the other hand the monastery, with its high walled courts and deep-browed cloisters, its noble refectory and vaulted kitchen, the herbarium or garden, shady with trees, and enriched with curious plants of Palestine, sloping down to the broad and majestic Thames, pure and blue as he pursued his silver winding way through emerald meadows and softly rising hills clothed with copses and woods. To the east, seated upon her hills, stood the crowned and battlemented city, the massive White Tower rising above the fortifications.

The autumn brilliance of October, 1269, never enlightened a more gorgeous scene than when it shone upon the ceremony still noted in our Calendar as the Translation of King Edward. Buried at first in his own low-browed heavy-arched Norman structure, which he had built, as he believed, at the express bidding of St. Peter; the Confessor, whose tender-hearted and devout nature had, by force of contrast with those of his fierce foreign successors, come to assume a saintly halo in the eyes not merely of the English, but of their Angevin lords themselves, was, now to reign on almost equal terms with the great Apostle himself, as one of the hallowing patrons of the Abbey—nay, since at least his relics were entire and undoubted, as its chief attraction.

The new chapel in his especial honour, behind the exquisite bayed apsidal chancel, was at length complete; and on this day he was to take possession of it. An ark of pure gold, chased and ornamented with the surpassing grace of that period of perfect taste, had received the royally robed corpse, which Churchmen averred lay calm and beautiful, untainted by decay; and this was now uplifted by the arms of King Henry himself, of Richard King of the Romans his brother, and of the two princes, Edward and Edmund.

It was a striking sight to see those two pairs of brothers. The two kings, nearly of an age, and so fondly attached that they could hardly brook a separation, till the death of the one broke the wearied heart of the other, were both gray-haired prematurely-aged men, of features that time instead of hardening had rendered more feeble and uncertain. Their faces were much alike, but Henry might be known from Richard by a certain inequality in the outline of his eyebrows; and their dress, though both alike wore long flowing gowns, the side seams only coming down as far as the thigh so as to allow play for the limbs, so far differed that Henry's was of blue, with the English lions embroidered in red and gold on his breast, and Richard was in the imperial purple, or rather scarlet, and the eagle of the empire on his breast testified to the futile election which he had purchased with the wealth of his Cornish mines. Both the elders together, with all their best will and their simple faith in the availing merit of the action they were performing, would have been physically incapable of proceeding many steps with their burden, but for the support it received from the two younger men who sustained the feet of the saint, using some dexterity in adapting their strength so that the coffin might be carried evenly.

One was the hunter we have already seen in Alton Wood. His features wore their characteristic stamp of deep awe and enthusiasm, and even as he slowly and calmly moved, sustaining the chief of the weight with scarcely an effort of his giant strength, his head towering high above all those around, his eyes might be observed to be seeing, though not marking, what was before them, but to be fixed as though the soul were in contemplation, far far away. He did not see in the present scene four princes rendering homage to a royal saint, who, from personal connection and by a brilliant display of devotion, might be propitiated into becoming a valuable patron amid intercessor; still less did it present itself to him as a pageant in which he was to bow his splendid powers, mental and bodily, to aid two feeble-minded old men to totter under the gold-cased corpse of a still more foolish and mischievous prince, dead two hundred years back. No, rather thought and eye were alike upon the great invisible world, the echo of whose chants might perchance be ringing on his ear; that world where holy kings cast their crowns before the Throne, and where the lamb-like spirit of the Confessor might be joining in the praise, and offering these tokens of honour to Him to whom all honour and praise and glory and blessing are due.

Of shorter stature, darker browed, of less regular feature and less clear complexion, so as to look as if he were the elder of the brothers, Prince Edmund moved by his side, using much exertion, and bending with the effort, so as to increase the slight sloop that had led to his historical nickname of the Crouchback, though some think this was merely taken from his crusading cross. He bore the arms of Sicily, to which he had not yet resigned his claim. His eye wandered, but not far away, like that of his brother. It was in search of his young betrothed, the Lady Aveline of Lancaster, the fair young heiress to whom he was to owe the great earldom that was a fair portion for a younger brother even of royalty.

All the four were bare-footed, and both princes were in robes much resembling that of their father, except that upon the left shoulder of each might be seen, in white cloth, the two lines of the Cross, that marked them as pilgrims and Crusaders, already on the eve of departure for the Holy Land.

The shrine where the golden coffin was to rest is substantially the same in our own day, with its triple-cusped arches below, the stage of six and stage of four above them, and the twisted columns in imitation of that which was supposed to have come from the Beautiful Gate of the Temple. But at that time it was a glittering fabric of mosaic work, in gold, lapis-lazuli, and precious stones, aided here and there by fragments of coloured glass, the only part of the costly workmanship that has come down to us. Around this shrine the preceding members of the procession had taken their places. Archbishop Boniface of Savoy was there, old age ennobling a countenance that once had been light and frivolous, and all his bishops in the splendour of their richest copes, solidly embroidered with absolute scenes and portraits in embroidery, with tall mitres worked with gold wire and jewels, and crosiers of beauteous workmanship in gold, ivory, and enamel. Mitred abbots, no less glorious in array, stood in another rank; the scarlet-mantled Grand Prior of the Hospital, and the white-cloaked Templar, made a link between the ecclesiastic and the warrior. Priests and monks, selected for their voices' sake, clustered in every available space; and, in full radiance, on a stage on the further side, were seated the ladies of the court, mostly with their hair uncovered, and surrounded by a garland of precious stones. Queen Eleanor of Provence, still bent on youthfulness, looked somewhat haggard in this garb; but it well became Beatrix von Falkmorite, the young German girl whom Richard King of the Romans had wedded in his old age for the sake of her fair face.

Smiling, plump, and rosy, she sat opening her wide blue eyes, wearing her emerald and ruby wreath as though it had been a coronal of daisies, and gazing with childish whisperings as she watched the movements of her king, and clung for direction and help in her own part of the pageant to the Princess Eleanor, who sat beside her, little the elder in years, less beautiful in colouring, but how far surpassing her in queenly pensive grace and dignity! Leaning on Eleanor's lap was a bright-eyed, bright-haired boy of four years old, watching with puzzled looks the brilliant ceremony, which he only half understood, and his glances wandering between his father and the blue and white robed little acolytes who stood nearest to the shrine, holding by chains the silver censers, which from time to time sent forth a fragrant vapour, curling round the heads of the nearest figures, and floating away in the lofty vaultings of the roof.

The actual ceremony could only be beheld by a favoured few; the official clergy, the many connections of royalty, and the chief nobility, filled the church to overflowing, but the rest of the world repaid itself by making a magnificent holiday. Good-natured King Henry had been permitted by his son, who had now, though behind the scenes, assumed the reins of government, to spend freely, and make a feast to his heart's content. Roasting and boiling were going on on a fast and furious scale, not only in the palace and abbey, but in booths erected in the fields; and tables were spreading and rushes strewing for the accommodation of all ranks. Near the entrance of the Abbey, the trains of the personages within awaited their coming forth in some sort of order, the more reverent listening to the sounds from within, and bending or crossing themselves as the familiar words of higher notes of praise rose loud enough to reach their ears; but for the most part, the tones and gestures were as various as the appearance of the attendants. Here were black Benedictines, there white Augustinians clustered round the sleek mules of their abbots; there scornful dark Templars, in their black and white, sowed the seeds of hatred against their order, and scarlet Hospitaliers looked bright and friendly even while repelling the jostling of the crowd. A hoary old squire, who had been with the King through all his troubles, kept together his immediate attendants; a party of boorish-looking Germans waited for Richard of Cornwall; and the slender, richly-caparisoned palfreys of the ladies were in charge of high-born pages, who sometimes, with means fair or foul, pushed back the throng, sometimes themselves became enamoured of its humours.

For not only had the neighbouring city of London poured forth her merchants and artizans, to gaze, wonder, and censure the extravagance—not only had beggars of every degree been attracted by the largesse that Henry delighted to dispense, and peasants had poured in from all the villages around, but no sort of entertainment was lacking. Here were minstrels and story-tellers gathering groups around them; here was the mountebank, clearing a stage in which to perform feats of jugglery, tossing from one hand to another a never- ending circle of balls, balancing a lance upon his nose, with a popinjay on its point; here were a bevy of girls with strange garments fastened to their ankles, who would dance on their hands instead of their feet, while their uplifted toes jangled little bells.

Peasant and beggar, citizen and performer, sightseer and professional, all alike strove to get into the space before the great entrance, where the procession must come forth to gratify the eyes of the gazers, and mayhap shower down such bounty as the elder mendicants averred had been given when Prince Edward (the saints defend him!) had been weighed at five years old, and, to avert ill luck, the counterbalance of pure gold had been thrown among the poor to purchase their prayers.

His weight in gold at his present stature could hardly be expected by the wildest imaginations, but hungry eyes had been estimating the weight of his little heir, and discontented lips had declared that the child was of too slender make to be ever worth so much to them as his father. Yet a whisper of the possibility had quickly been magnified to a certainty of such a largesse, and the multitude were thus stimulated to furious exertions to win the most favourable spot for gathering up such a golden rain as even little Prince Henry's counterpoise would afford; and ever as time waxed later, the throng grew denser and more unruly, and the struggle fiercer and more violent.

The screams and expostulations of the weak, elbowed and trampled down, mingled with more festive sounds; and the attendants who waited on the river in the large and beautifully-ornamented barges which were the usual conveyances of distinguished personages, began to agree with one another that if they saw less than if they were on the bank, they escaped a considerable amount of discomfort as well as danger.

"For," murmured one of the pages, "I suppose it would be a dire offence to the Prince to lay about among the churls as they deserve."

"Ay, truly, among Londoners above all," was the answer of his companion, whom the last four years had rendered considerably taller than when we saw him last.

"Not that there is much love lost between them. He hath never forgotten the day when they pelted the Queen with rotten eggs, and sang their ribald songs; nor they the day he rode them down at Lewes like corn before the reaper."

"And lost the day," muttered the other page; then added, "The less love, the more cause for caution."

"Oh yes, we know you are politic, Master Richard," was the sneering reply, "but you need not fear my quarrelling with your citizen friends. I would not be the man to face Prince Edward if I had made too free with any of the caitiffs."

"Hark! Master Hamlyn, the tumult is louder than ever," interposed an elderly man of lower rank, who was in charge of the stout rowers in the royal colours of red and gold. "Young gentlemen, the Mass must be ended; it were better to draw to the stairs, than to talk of you know not what," he muttered.

Hamlyn de Valence, who held the rudder, steered towards the wide stone steps that descended to the river, nearest to the apse in which "St. Peter's Abbey Church" terminated before Henry VII. had added his chapel. At that moment a louder burst of sound, half imprecation, half shriek, was heard; there was a heavy splash a little way above, and a small blue bundle was seen on the river, apparently totally unheeded by the frantic crowd on the bank. No sooner was it seen by Richard, however, than he threw back his mantle and sprang out of the barge. There was a loud cry from the third page, a little fellow of nine or ten years old; but Richard gallantly swam out, battled with the current, and succeeded in laying hold of a young child, with whom he made for the barge, partly aided by the stream; but he was breathless, and heartily glad to reach the boat and support himself against the gunwale.

"A pretty boat companion you!" said Hamlyn maliciously. "How are we to take you in, over the velvet cushions?"

The little page gave an expostulating cry.

"Hold the child an instant, John," gasped Richard, raising it towards his younger friend; "I will but recover breath, and then land and seek out her friends."

"How is this?" said a voice above them; and looking up, they found that while all had been absorbed in the rescue, the Prince, with his little son in his arms and his wife hanging on his arm, had come to the stone stairs, and was looking down. "Richard overboard!"

"A child fell over the bank, my Lord," eagerly shouted the little John, with cap in hand, "and he swam out to pick it up."

"Into the barge instantly, Richard," commanded the Prince. "'Tis as much as his life is worth to remain in this cold stream!"

And truly Richard was beginning to feel as much. He was assisted in by two of the oarsmen, and the barge then putting towards the steps, the Princess was handed into her place, and began instantly to ask after the poor child. It had not been long enough in the water to lose its consciousness, though it had hitherto been too much frightened to cry; but it no sooner opened a wide pair of dark eyes to find itself in strange hands, than it set up a lamentable wail, calling in broken accents for "Da-da."

"Let me take it ashore at once, gracious lady," said Richard, revived by a draught of wine from the stores provided for the long day; "I will find its friends."

"Nay," said the Princess, "it were frenzy to take it thus in its wet garments; and frenzy to remain in thine, Richard." As she spoke, the Prince and the other persons of the suite had embarked, and the barge was pushing away from the steps. "Give the child to me," she added, holding out her arms, and disregarding a remonstrance from one of her ladies, disregarding too the sobs and struggles of the child, whom she strove to soothe, while hastily removing the little thing's soaked blue frock and hood, and wrapping it up in a warm woollen cloak. "It is a pretty little maiden," she said, "and not ill cared for. Some mother's heart must be bursting for her!— Hush thee! hush thee, little one; we will take thee home and clothe thee, and then thou shalt go to thy mother," she added, in better English than she had spoken four years earlier in Alton Wood. But the child still cried for her da-da, and the Princess asked again, "What is thy father's name, little maid?"

"Pere," she answered, with a peculiar accent that made the Prince say, "That is a Provencal tongue."

"They are Provencal eyes likewise," added Eleanor. "See how like their hue is to Richard's own;" and in Provencal she repeated the question what the father's name and the child's own might be. But "Pere" again, and "Bessee, pretty Bessee," was all the answer she obtained, the last in unmistakable English.

"I thought," said Eleanor, "that it was only my own children that scarce knew whether they spoke English, Languedoc, or Langued'oui."

"It was the same with us, Lady," said Richard. "Father Adam was wont to say we were a little Babel."

The child looked towards him on hearing his voice, and held out her hands to go to him, reiterating an entreaty to be taken to her father.

"She is probably the child of some minstrel or troubadour," said the Prince. "We will send in search of him as soon as we have reached the Savoy."

The Savoy Palace had been built for Queen Eleanor's obnoxious uncle, Prince Thomas of Savoy, and had recently been purchased by the Queen herself, as a wedding gift for her son Edmund; but in the meantime Edward and his family were occupying it during their stay near Westminster, and their barge was brought up to the wide stairs of its noble court. Richard was obliged to give up the child to the Princess and her ladies, though she shrieked after him so pertinaciously, that Eleanor called to him to return so soon as he should have changed his garments.

In a few minutes he again appeared, and found the little girl dressed in a little garment of one of the royal children, but totally insensible to the honour, turning away from all the dainties offered to her, and sobbing for her father, much to the indignation of the two little princes, Henry and John, who stood hand in hand staring at her. She flew to him directly, with a broken entreaty that she might be taken to her father. Again they tried questioning her, but Richard, whether speaking English or Provencal, always succeeded in obtaining readier and more comprehensible replies than did the Princess. Whether she recognized him as her preserver, or whether his language had a familiar tone, she seemed exclusively attracted by him; and he it was who learnt that she lived at home—far off—on the Green near the red monks, and that her father could not see—he would be lost without Bessee to lead him. And the little creature, hardly three years old if so much, was evidently in the greatest trouble at her father having lost her guidance and protection.

Richard, touched and flattered by the little maiden's exclusive preference, and owning in her Provencal eyes and speech something strangely like his own young sister Eleanor, entreated permission to be himself the person to take her in search of her friends. The Princess added her persuasions, declaring it would be cruel to send the poor little thing with another stranger, and that his Provencal tongue was needed in order to discovering her father among the troubadours.

Edward yielded to her persuasion, adding, however, that Richard must take two men-at-arms with him, and gravely bidding him be on his guard. Nor would he permit him to be accompanied by little John de Mohun, who, half page, half hostage, had lately been added to the Princess's train, and being often bullied and teased by Hamlyn and his fellows, had vehemently attached himself to Richard, and now entreated in vain to go with him on the adventure. In fact, Prince Edward was a stern disciplinarian, equally severe against either familiarity or insolence towards the external world, and especially towards any one connected with London. If Richard ever gave him any offence, it was by a certain freedom of manner towards inferiors, such as the Earl of Leicester had diligently inculcated on his family, but which more than once had excited a shade of vexation on the Prince's part. Even after Richard had reached the door, he was called back and commanded on no pretext to loiter or enter on any dispute, and if his search should detain him late, to sleep at the Tower, rather than be questioned and stopped at any of the gates which were guarded at night by the citizens.

CHAPTER V—THE OLD KNIGHT OF THE HOSPITAL

"The warriors of the sacred grave,
  Who looked to Christ for laws."
Lord Houghton.

Richard summoned a small boat, and with two stout men-at-arms, of whom Adam de Gourdon was one, prepared again to cross the river. Leonillo ran down the stone stairs with a wistful look of entreaty and it occurred to both Richard and Adam, that, could the child only lead them to the place where her father had sat, the dog's scent might prove their most efficient guide.

Little Bessee seemed quite comforted when on her way back to her father, and sat on Richard's knee, eating the comfits with which the Princess had provided her, and making him cut a figure that seemed somewhat to amaze the other boat-loads whom they encountered on the river.

When they landed, the throng was more dispersed, but revelry and sports of all kinds were going on fast and furiously; each door of the Abbey was besieged by hungry crowds receiving their dole, and Richard's inquiries for a blind man who had lost his child were little heeded, or met with no satisfactory answer. Bessee herself was bewildered, and incapable of finding her father's late station; and Richard was becoming perplexed, and doubtful whether he ought to take her back, as well as somewhat put out of countenance by the laughter of Thomas de Clare, and other young nobles, who rallied him on his strange charge.

At last the little girl's face lightened as at sight of something familiar. "Good red monks," she said. "They give Bessee soup—make father well."

With a ray of hope, Richard advanced to a party of Brethren of St. John, who were mounting at the Abbey gate to return to their house at Spitalfields, and doffing his bonnet, intimated a desire to address the tall old war-worn knight with a benevolent face, who was adjusting his scarlet cloak, before mounting a gray Arab steed looking as old and worthy as himself.

"Ha! a young Crusader, I perceive," was the greeting of the old knight, as his eye fell on the white cross on Richard's mantle. "Welcome, brother! Dost thou need counsel on thy goodly Eastern way?"

"Thanks, reverend Sir," returned Richard, "but my present purpose was to seek for the father of this little one, who fell into the river in the press. She

34

pointed to you, saying she had received your bounty."

"It is Blind Hal's child, Sir Robert!" exclaimed a serving-brother in black, coming eagerly forward; "the villeins on the green told me the poor knave was distraught at having lost his child in the throng!"

"What brought he her there for?" exclaimed Sir Robert. "Poor fool! his wits must have forsaken him!"

"The child had a craving to see the show," replied the Brother, "so Hob the cobbler told me; and all went well till my Lord of Pembroke's retainers forced all right and left to make way in the crowd. Hal was thrown down, and the child thrust away till they feared she had fallen over the bank. Hob and his wife were fain to get the poor man away, for his moans and fierce words were awful: and he was not a little hurt in the scuffle, so I e'en gave them leave to lay him in the cart that brought up your reverence's vestments, and the gear we lent the Abbey for the show."

"Right, Brother Hilary," said Sir Robert; "and now the poor knave will have his best healing.—He must have been a good soldier once," he added to Richard; "but he is a mere fragment of a man, wasted in your Earl of Leicester's wars."

"Where dwells he?" asked Richard, keenly interested in all his father's old followers; "I would fain restore him his child."

"In a hut on Bednall Green," answered the serving-brother; "but twice or thrice a week he comes to the Spital to have his hurts looked to."

"Ay! we tell him his little witch must soon be shut out! She turns the heads of all our brethren," said Sir Robert, smiling. "Wild work she makes with our novices."

"Wilder with our Knights Commanders, maybe, Sir," retorted, laughing, a fair open-faced youth in his novitiate. "I shall some day warn Hal how our brethren, the Templars, are said to play at ball with tender babes on their lances."

"No scandal about our brethren of the Temple, Rayland," said Sir Robert, looking grave for a moment.—"Young Sir, it would be a favour if you would ride with us; we would gladly show you the way to Bednall Green."

"I should rejoice to go, Sir," returned Richard, "but I am of Prince Edward's household—Richard Fowen; and my horse is on the other side of the river."

"That is soon remedied," said Sir Robert, who seemed to have taken a great fancy to Richard, either for the sake of his crossed shoulder, or of his kindness to the little plaything of the Spital. "Our young brother, Engelbert von Fuchstein, has leave to tarry this night with his brother in the train of the King of the Romans, and his horse is at your service, if you will do our poor Spital the favour to tarry there this night, and ride it back in the morn to meet him at Westminster."

Richard knew that this invitation might be safely accepted without danger of giving umbrage to the Prince, who was on the best terms with the Knights of the Hospital. He therefore dismissed Gourdon and the other man-at-arms with a message explaining the matter; and warmly thanking the old Grand Prior, laid one hand on the saddle of the great ponderous beast that was led up to him, and vaulted on its back without touching the stirrup.

"Well done, my young master," said Sir Robert, "it is easy to see you are of the Prince's household."

"I cannot yet do as the Prince can," said Richard,—"take this leap in full armour."

"No; and let me give you a bit of counsel, fair Sir. Such pastimes are very well for the tiltyard, but they should be laid aside in the blessed Land, and strength reserved for the one cause and purpose." He crossed himself; and in the meantime, Bessee intimated her imperious purpose of not riding before Brother Hilary, but being perched before Richard on the enormous cream-coloured animal, whence he was looking down from a considerable elevation upon Sir Robert on his slender Arab.

"These are the German monsters that our brethren bring over," said Sir Robert. "Mark me, young brother, cumber not yourself with these beasts of Europe, which are good for nothing but food for foul birds in the East. Purvey yourself of an Arab as soon as you land. There is a rogue at Acre, one Ali by name, who will not cheat you more than is reasonable, so you mention my name to him, Sir Robert Darcy, at your service."

"Thanks, reverend Father," returned Richard, "but I am but a landless page, and the Prince mounts me. Said you this poor man had been wounded in the late wars?"

"Ay, hacked and hewed worse than by the Infidels themselves! Woeful it is that here, at home, men's blood should be wasted on your own petty feuds. This same Barons' war now hath cost as much downright courage as would have brought us back to Jerusalem, and all thrown away, without a cause, with no honour, no hope."

"Not without a cause," Richard could not help saying.

"Nay," said the old knight; "no cause is worth the taking of a life, save the cause of the Holy Sepulchre. What be these matters of taxes and laws to ask a man to shed his blood for? Alack, the temper of the cross-bearer is dying out! I pray I may not see this Crusade end like half those I have beheld—and the cross on the shoulder become no better than a mockery."

"That may scarcely be with such leaders as the Prince and the King of France," said Richard.

"Well, well, the Prince is untried; and for King Louis, he is as holy a man as ever lived since King Godfrey of blessed memory, but he has bad luck, ever bad luck. The Saints forefend, but I trow he will listen to some crazy counsel from Rome, belike, or some barefooted hermit—very holy, no doubt, but who does not know a Greek from a Saracen, or a horse's head from his tail—and will go to some pestilential hole like that foul Egyptian swamp, where we stayed till our skin was the colour of an old boot, in hopes of converting the Sultan of Babylon, or the Old Man of the Mountain, or what not, and there he will stay till the flower of his forces have wasted away."

"Were you in Egypt with King Louis?" eagerly exclaimed Richard.

"Ay, marry, was I, and a goodly land it is; but I saw many a good man-at-arms perish miserably in a marsh, who might have been the saving of the Holy City. Why, I myself have never been the same man since! Never could do a month's service out of the infirmary at Acre, though after all there's no work I like so well as the hospital business, and for the last five years I have had to stay here training young brethren! Oh, young man! I envy you your first stroke for the Holy Sepulchre! Would that the Grand-Master would hear my entreaty. I am too old to be worth sparing, and I would fain have one more chance of dying under the banner of the Order!—But I am setting you a bad example, son Raynal; a Hospitalier has no will.- -And look you, young Sir Page, if you stay out at sunset in that clime, 'tis all up with you. And you should veil your helmet well, or the sun smites on your head as deadly as a flake of Greek fire."

So rambled on good old Sir Robert Darcy, Grand Prior of England, a perfect dragon among the Saracens, but everywhere else the mildest and most benevolent of men; his discourse strangely mingling together the deepest enthusiasm with a business-like common-sense appreciation of ways and means, and with minute directions, precautions, and anecdotes, gathered from his practical experience both as captain in the field, priest in the Church, and surgeon in the hospital, and all seen from the most sunshiny point of view.

Meanwhile, they were riding along the Strand, a beautiful open road, with grassy borders shelving down to the Thames. They passed through the City of London. The Hospital lay beyond the walls, but the Marshes of Moorfields that protected them were not passable without a long circuit; and the fortified gates stood open at Temple Bar, where the Hospitaliers, looking towards the Round Church and stately buildings of the Preceptory, saluted the white-cloaked figures moving about it, with courtesy grim and distant in all but Sir Robert Darcy, who could not even hate a Templar, a creature to the ordinary Hospitalier far more detestable than a Saracen. On then, up ground beginning to rise, below which the little muddy stream called the Flete stagnated along its way, meandering to the Thames. Thatched hovels and wooden booths left so narrow a passage that the horsemen were forced to move in single file, and did not gain a clearer space even when the stone houses of merchants began to stand thick on Ludgate Hill, their carved wooden balconies so projecting, that it would seem to have been an object with the citizens to be able to shake hands across the street. The city was comparatively empty and quiet, as all the world were keeping holiday at Westminster; but even as it was, the passengers seemed to swarm in the streets, and knots of persons who had been unable to witness the spectacle, sat with gazing children upon the stairs outside the houses, to admire the fragments of the pageant that came their way. Acclamations of delight greeted the appearance of the scarlet-mantled Hospitaliers, such as Richard had often heard in his boyhood, when riding in his father's train, but far less frequently since he had been a part of the Prince's retinue. And equally diverse was the merry nod and smile of Sir Robert to each gaping shouting group of little ones, from the stately distant courtesy with which Edward returned the popular salutations. He could be gracious—he could not be friendly except to a few.

They passed the capitular buildings of St. Paul's, with the beautiful cathedral towering over them, and in its rear, numerous booths for the purchase of rosaries—recent inventions then of St. Dominic, the great friend of Richard's stern grandfather, the persecutor of the Albigenses. Sir Robert drew up, and declared he must buy one for the little maid as a remembrance of the day, and then found she was fast asleep; but he nevertheless purchased a black-beaded chaplet, giving for it one of the sorely-clipped coins of King Henry.

"Prithee let me have one likewise, holy Sir," quoth Richard, "in memory of the talk that hath taught me so much of the import of my crusading vow."

"Thou shalt bring me for it one of the olive of Bethlehem," said Sir Robert; "I have given away all I brought from the East. They are so great a boon to our poor sick folk that I wish I had brought twice as many, but to me they have always a Saracen look. Your Moslem always fingers one much of the same fashion as he parleys."

Ludgate, freshly built, and adorned with new figures to represent the fabulous King Lud, was not yet closed for the night; and the party came forth beyond the walls, with the desolate Moorfields to their left, and before them a number of rising villages clustered round their churches.

The Hospital, a grand fortified monastery, was already to be seen over the fields; but Sir Robert, sending home the rest of his troop, turned aside with Richard and Brother Hilary towards the common, with a border of cottages around it, which went by the name of Bednall Green.

Brother Hilary knew the hut inhabited by Blind Hal, and led the way to it. Low and mud-built, thatched, and with a wattled door, it had a wretched appearance; but the old woman who came to the door was not ill clad. "Blessings on you, holy Father!" she cried; "do I see the child, my lamb, my lady-bird! Would that she may come in time to cheer her poor father!"

"How is it with him then, Gammer?" demanded Sir Robert, springing to the ground with the alacrity of a doctor anxious about his patient.

"Ill, very ill, Sir. Whether the horse's feet hurt his old wound, or whether it be the loss of the child, he hath done nought but moan and rave, and lie as one dead ever since they brought him home. He is lying in one of the dead swoons now! It were not well that the child saw him."

But Bessee, awakening with a cry of joy, saw her borne, and struggled to go to her father, whose name she called on with all her might, disregarding the caresses of the old woman, and the endeavour made by Richard to restrain without alarming her, while Sir Robert went into the hut to endeavour to restore the sufferer.

Suddenly a cry broke from within; and Richard, turning at the voice, beheld the blind man sitting up on his pallet with arms outstretched. "My child!—My Father! hast thou brought her to visit me in limbo?" he cried.

"He raves!" said Richard, using his strength to withhold the child, who broke out into a shriek.

"Nay, nay! she doth not abide here!" he exclaimed. "Her spirit is pure! My sins are not visited on her beyond the grave!"

"Thou art on the earthly side of the grave still, my son," said Sir Robert, at the same time as Bessee sprang from Richard, and nestled on his breast, clinging to his neck.

"My babe—my Bessee!" he exclaimed, gathering her close to him. "Living, living, indeed! Yet how may it be! Surely this is the other world. That voice sounds not among the living!"

"It is the voice of the youth who saved thy child," said the Grand Prior.

"Speak again! Let him speak again!" implored the beggar.

"Can I do aught for you, good man?" asked Richard.

Again there was a strange start and thrill of amazement.

"Only for Heaven's sake tell me who thou art!"

"A page of Prince Edward's good man. I am called Richard Fowen! And who, for Heaven's sake, are you?" added Richard, as Leonillo, who had been smelling about and investigating, threw himself on the blind man in a transport of caresses. "Off, Leon—off!" cried Richard. "It is but a dog!—Fear not, little one!—Tell me, tell me," he added, trembling, as he knelt before the miserable object, holding back the eager Leonillo with one arm round his neck, "who art thou, thou ghost of former times?"

"Knowst me not, Richard?" returned a suppressed voice in Provencal.

"Henry! Henry!" exclaimed Richard, and fell upon the foot of the low bed, weeping bitterly. "Is it come to this?"

"Ay, even to this," said the blind man, "that two sons of one father meet unknown—one with a changed name, the other with none at all, neither with the honoured one they were born to."

"Alack, alack!" was all Richard could say at the first moment, as he lifted himself up to look again at the first-born of his parents, the head of the brave troop of brethren, the gay, handsome, imperious young Lord de Montfort, whose proud head and gallant bearing he had looked at with a younger brother's imitative deference. What did he see but a wreck of a man, sitting crouched on the wretched bed, the left arm a mere stump, a bandage where the bright sarcastic eyes used to flash forth their dark fire, deep scars on all the small portion of the face that was visible through the over-grown masses of hair and beard, so plentifully sprinkled with white, that it would have seemed incredible that this man was but eight months older than the Prince, whose rival he had always been in personal beauty and activity. The beautiful child, clasped close to his breast, her face buried on his shoulder under his shaggy locks, was a strange contrast to his appearance, but only added to the look of piteous helplessness and desolation, as she hung upon him in her alarm at the agitation around her.

Richard had long been accustomed to think of his brother as dead; but such a spectacle as this was far more terrible to him, and his cheek blanched at the shock, as he gasped again, "Thou here, and thus! thou whom I thought slain!"

"Deem me so still," said his brother, "even as I deem the royal minion dead to me."

"Nay, Henry, thou knowst not."

"Who is present?" interrupted the blind man, raising his head and tossing back his hair with a gesture that for the first time gave Richard a sense that his eldest brother was indeed before him. "Methought I heard another voice."

"I am here, fair son," replied the old knight, "Father Robert of the Hospital! I will either leave thee, or keep thy secret as though it were thy shrift; but thou art sore spent, and mayst scarce talk more."

"Weariness and pain are past, Father, with my little one again in my bosom," said Henry; "and there are matters that must be spoken between me and this young brother of mine ere he quits this hut; and his voice resumed its old authoritative tone towards Richard. "Said you that he had saved my child?"

"He drew me from the river, Father," said Bessee looking up. "There was nothing to stand on, and it was so cold! And he took me in his arms and pulled me out, and put me in a boat; and the lady pulled off my blue coat, and put this one on me. Feel it, Father; oh, so pretty, so warm!"

"It was the Princess," said Richard; but Henry, not noticing, continued,

"Thou hast earned my pardon, Richard," and held out his remaining hand, somewhere towards the height where his brother's used to be.

Sir Robert smiled, saying, "Thou dost miscalculate thy brother's stature, son." And at the same moment Richard, who was now little short of his Cousin Edward in height, was kneeling by Henry, accepting and returning his embrace with agitation and gratitude, such as showed how their relative positions in the family still maintained their force; but Richard still asserted his independence so as to say, "When you have heard all, brother you will see that there is no need of pardoning me."

Henry, however, as perhaps Sir Robert had foreseen, instead of answering put his hand to his side, and sank back in a paroxysm of pain, ending in another swoon. The child stood by, quiet and frightened but too much used to similar occurrences to be as much terrified as was Richard, who thought his brother dying; but calling in the serving-brother, the old Hospitalier did all that was needed, and the blind man presently recovered and explained in a feeble voice that he had been jostled, thrown down, and trodden on, at the moment when he lost his hold of his little daughter; and this was evidently renewing his sufferings from the effect of an injury received in battle. "And what took thee there, son?" said Sir Robert, somewhat sharply.

"The harvest, Father," answered Henry, rousing himself to speak with a certain sarcasm in his tone. "It is the beggars' harvest wherever King Henry goes. We brethren of the wallet cannot afford to miss such windfalls."

"A beggar!" exclaimed Richard in horror.

"And what art thou?" retorted Henry, with a sudden fierceness.

"Listen, young men," said Sir Robert, "this I know, my patient there will soon be nothing if ye continue in this strain. A litter shall bring him to the infirmary."

"Nay," said Henry hastily, "not so, good Father. Here I abide, hap what may."

"And I abide with him," said Richard.

"Not so, I say," returned the Hospitalier, "unless thou wouldst slay him outright. Return to the Spital with me; and at morn, if he have recovered himself, unravel these riddles as thou and he will."

"It is well, Father," said Henry. "Go with him, Richard; but mark me. Be silent as the grave, and see me again."

And reluctant as he was, Richard was forced to comply.

CHAPTER VI—THE BEGGAR EARL

"Along with the nobles that fell at that tyde,
His eldest son Henrye, who fought by his syde,
Was felde by a blow he receivde in the fight;
A blow that for ever deprivde him of sight."
Old Beggar.

The chapel at the Spital was open to all who chose to attend. The deep choir was filled with the members of the Order, half a dozen knights in the stalls, and the novices and serving-brothers so ranged as to give full effect to the body of voice. Richard knelt on the stone floor outside the choir, intending after early mass to seek his brother; but to his surprise he found the blind man with his child at his feet in what was evidently his accustomed place, just within the door. His hair and beard were now arranged, his appearance was no longer squalid; but when he rose to depart, guided in part by the child, but also groping with a stick, he looked even more helpless than on his bed, and Richard sprang forward to proffer an arm for his support.

"Flemish cloth and frieze gown," said the object of his solicitude in a strange gibing voice; "court page and street beggar—how now, my master?"

"Lord Earl and elder brother," returned Richard, "thine is my service through life."

"Mine? Ho, ho! That much for thy service!" with a disdainful gesture of his fingers. "A strapping lad like thee would be the ruin of my trade. I might as well give up bag and staff at once."

"Nay, surely, wilt thou not?" exclaimed Richard in broken words from his extreme surprise. "The King and Prince only long to pardon and restore, and —"

"And thou wouldst well like to lord it at Kenilworth, earl in all but the name? Thou mayst do so yet without being cumbered with me or mine!"

"Thou dost me wrong, Henry," said Richard, much distressed. "I love the Prince, for none so truly honoured our blessed father as he, and for his sake he hath been most kind lord to me; but thou art the head of my house, my brother, and with all my heart do I long to render thee such service as—as may lighten these piteous sufferings."

"I believe thee, Richard; thou wert ever an honest simple-hearted lad," said Henry, in a different tone; "but the only service thou canst render me is to let me alone, and keep my secret. Here—I feel that we are at the stone bench, where I bask in the sun, and lay out my dish for the visitors of the gracious Order.—Here, Bessee, child, put the dish down," he added, retaining his hold of his brother, as if to feel whether Richard winced at this persistence in his strange profession. The little girl obeyed, and betook herself to the quiet sports of a lonely child, amusing herself with Leonillo, and sometimes returning to her father and obtaining his attention for a few moments, sometimes prattling to some passing brother of the Order, who perhaps made all the more of the pretty creature because this might be called an innocent breach of discipline. "And now, Master Page," said Henry in his tone of authority, yet with some sarcasm, "let us hear how long-legged Edward finished the work he had began on thee at Hereford—made thee captive in the battle, eh?"

Richard briefly narrated his life with Gourdon, and his capture by the Prince, adding, "My mother was willing I should remain with him; she bade me do anything rather than join Simon and Guy; and verily, brother, save that the Prince is less free of speech, his whole life seems moulded upon our blessed father's—"

"Speak not of them in the same breath," cried Henry hastily. "And wherefore —if such be his honour to him whom he slew and mutilated— art thou to disown thy name, and stand before him like some chance foundling?"

"That was the King's doing," said Richard. "The Prince was averse to it, but

King Henry, though he wept over me and called me his dear nephew, made it his special desire that he might not hear the name of Montfort; and the Prince, though overruling him in all that pertains to matters of state, is most dutiful in all lesser matters. I hoped at least to be called Fitz Simon, but some mumble of the King turned it into Fowen, and so it has continued. I believe no one at court is really ignorant of my lineage; but among the people, Montfort is still a trumpet-call, and the King fears to hear it."

"Well he may!" laughed Henry. "Rememberest thou, Richard, the sorry figure our good uncle cut, when we armed him so courteously, and put him on his horse to meet the rebels at Evesham—how he durst not hang back, and loved still less to go onward, and kept calling me his loving nephew all the time?"

"Ah! Henry—but didst thou not hear my father mutter, when he saw the crowned helm under the standard, that it was ill done, and no good could come of seething the kid in the mother's milk? And verily, had not the Prince been carrying his father from the field, I trow the Mortimers had not refused us quarter, nor had their cruel will of us."

"Oh ho! thou art come to have opinions of thine own!" laughed Henry, with the scoff of a senior unable to brook that his younger brother should think for himself. Yet this tone was so familiar to Richard's ears, that it absolutely encouraged him to a nearer step to intimacy. He said, "But how scapedst thou, Henry? I could have sworn that I saw thee fall, skull and helmet cleft, a dead man!"

Instead of answering, Henry put his hand under the chin of his child, who was leaning against him, and holding up her face to his brother, said, "Thou canst see this child's face? Tell me what like she is."

"Like little Eleanor, like Amaury. The home-look of her eyes won my heart at once. Even the Princess remarked their resemblance to mine. Think of Eleanor and thy mind's eye will see her."

"No other likeness?" said the blind man wistfully; "but no—thou wast at Hereford when she was at Odiham."

"Who?"

He grasped Richard's hand, and under his breath uttered the name "Isabel."

"Isabel Mortimer!" exclaimed Richard, who had been, of course, aware of his brother's betrothal, when the two families of Montfort and Mortimer had been on friendly terms; "we heard she had taken the veil!"

"And so thou sawst me slain!" said Henry de Montfort dryly.

"But how—how was it?" asked Richard eagerly.

"Men sometimes tie knots faster than they intend," said Henry. "When Roger Mortimer took Simon's doings in wrath, and vowed that his sister should never wed a Montfort, he knew not what he did. He and his proud wife could flout and scorn my Isabel—they might not break her faith to me. Thou knowst, perhaps, Richard, since thou art hand and glove with our foes, that like a raven to the slaughter, the Lady Mortimer came as near the battle-field as her care for her dainty person would allow; and there was one whom she brought with her. And, gentle dame, what doth she do but carry her sister-in-law a sweet and womanly gift? What thinkst thou it was, Richard?"

"I fear I know," said Richard, choked; "my father's hand."

"Nay, that was a choicer morsel reserved for my lady countess herself. It was mine own, with our betrothal-ring thereon. Now, quoth that loving sister, might Isabel resume her ring. No plighted troth could be her excuse any longer for refusing to wed my Lord of Gloucester. Then rose up my love, 'It beckons me!' she said, and bade them leave it with her. They deemed that it was for death that it beckoned. So mayhap did she. I wot Countess Maud had little grieved. But little dreamed they of her true purpose—my perfect jewel of constant love—namely, to restore the lopped hand to the poor corpse, that it might likewise have Christian burial. Her old nurse, Welsh Winny, was as true to her as she was to me; and forth they sped, fearless of the spoilers, and made their way at nightfall even to the Abbey Church, where Edward, less savage than the fair countess, had caused us to be laid before the altar, awaiting our burial in the vaults."

"Thou wert senseless all this time?"

"Ay, and so continued. The pang when my hand was severed had roused me for a few moments, but only to darkness; and my effort to speak had been rewarded with as many Welsh knives as could pierce my flesh at once."

"And thou didst not bleed to death?"

"The swoon checked my blood. And the monks of Evesham must have staunched and bandaged so as to make a decent corpse of me. Had they had a man-at-arms among them, they would have known that mine were not the wounds of a dead but of a living man. The old nurse knew it, when my sweet lady would needs unbind my wrist, to place my hand in its right place. An old crone such as Welsh Winny never stirs without her cordial potion. They poured it into my lips—and if I were never more to awake to the light of day, I awoke to the sound that was yet dearer to me—while, alas! it still was left to me."

He became silent, till Richard's question drew him on.

"What with their care and support, when once on my feet I found strength to stumble out of the chapel and gain shelter in the woods ere day; and I believe the monks got credit for their zeal in casting out the excommunicate body."

"Not credit," said Richard; "the Prince was full of grief, more especially as they all disavowed the deed. But, brother, art thou excommunicate still?"

"Far from it, most pious Crusader. If seas of holy wells could assoil me, I should be pure enough. My sweet Isabel deemed that some such washing might bring back mine eyesight; and from one to another we wandered as my limbs could bear it. And at St. Winifred's there was a priest who told us strange tales of the miracles wrought in the Mortimer household by my father's severed hand; nay, that it had so worked on Lord Mortimer's sister, that she had left the vanities of the world, and gone into a nunnery. He seemed so convinced of my father's saintliness, and so honest a fellow, that Isabel insisted on unbosoming ourselves to him under seal of confession. No longer was the old nurse to be my mother and she my sister; and the good man made no difficulties, but absolved me, and wedded me to the truest, most loving wife that ever blessed a man bereft of all else."

"And you begged! O Henry, the noble lady—"

"At first we had the knightly chain and spurs in which the monks had kindly pranked me up. Isabel too had worn a few jewels; but after all, a palmer need never hunger. My father always said no trade was so well paid as begging, under King Henry, and verily we found it so. She used at times to gather berries and thread them for chaplets to sell at the holy wells; but I trow sheer beggary throve better!"

"But wherefore? Even had pardon not been ready, Simon held out Kenilworth for months."

Henry laughed his dry laugh.

"Simple boy, dost think I would trust Simon with an elder brother whose hand could no longer keep his head?"

"And my mother—"

"She had always hated the Mortimers, even when the contract was matter of policy. Would I have taken my sweet Isabel to abide her royal scorn, it might be incredulity of our marriage? Though for that matter it is more unimpeachable than her own! Nay, nay, out of ken and out of reach was our only security from our kin on either side, unless we desired that my head should follow my hand as a dainty dish for Countess Maud."

"How could the lady brook it?"

"She dyed her fair skin with walnut, wore russet gown and hood, and was a very nightingale for blitheness and sweet song through that first year," said Henry; "blither than ever when that little one was born in the sunshiny days of Whitsuntide. I tell thee, those were happier days than ever I passed as Lord de Montfort at Kenilworth. But after that, the bruised hurt in my side, which had never healed when the cleaner gashes did, became more painful and troublesome. Holy wells did nothing for it; and she wasted with watching it, as though my pain had been hers. Naught would serve her but coming here, because she had been told that the Knights of St. John had better experience of old battle-wounds than any men in the realm. Much ado had we to get here —the young babe in her arms, and I well- nigh distraught with pain. We crept into this same hut, and I had a weary sickness throughout the winter—living, I know not how, by the bounty of the Spital, and by the works of her fingers, which Winny would take out to sell on feast-days in the city. Oh that eyes had been left me to note how she pined away! but I had scarce felt how thin and bony were her tender fingers ere the blasts of the cruel March wind finished the work."

"Alack! alack! poor Henry," said Richard; "never, never was lady of romaunt so noble, and so true!"

"No more," said Henry hastily, leaning his brow on the top of his staff. "Come hither, Bessee," he added after a brief pause; "say thy prayer for thy blessed mother, child."

And holding out his one hand, he inclosed her two clasped ones within it, as the little voice ran over an utterly unintelligible form of childishly clipped Latin, sounding, however, sweet and birdlike from the very liberties the little memory had taken in twisting its mellifluous words into a rhythm of her own. And there was catchword enough for Richard to recognize and follow it, with bonnet doffed, and crossing himself.

"And now," he said, "surely the need for secrecy is ended. The land is tranquil, the King ruled by the Prince, the Prince owning all the past folly and want of faith that goaded our father into resistance. Wherefore not seek his willing favour? Thou art ever a pilgrim. Be with us in the crusade. Who knows what the Jordan waves may effect for thee?"

"No, no," grimly laughed Henry. "Dost think any favour would make it tolerable to be wept over and pitied by the King—pitied by THE KING," he repeated in ineffable disgust; "or to be the show of the court, among all that knew me of old, when I WAS a man? Hob the cobbler, and Martin the bagster, are better company than Pembroke and Gloucester, and I meet with more humours on Cheapside than I should at Winchester—more regard too. Why, they deem me threescore years old at least, and I am a very oracle of wisdom among them. Earl of Leicester, forsooth! he would be nobody compared with Blind Hal! And as to freedom—with child and staff the whole country and city are before me—no shouts to dull retainers, and jackanape pages to set my blind lordship on horseback, without his bridle hand, and lead him at their will anywhere but at his own.

"All this I can understand for thyself," said Richard; "but for thy child's sake canst thou not be moved?"

"My child, quotha? What, when her Uncle Simon is true grandson to King John?"

Richard started. "I cannot believe what thou sayest of Simon," he answered in displeasure.

"One day thou wilt," calmly answered Henry; "but I had rather not have it proved upon the heiress of Leicester and Montfort."

"Leicester is forfeit—Simon an outlawed man."

"If the humour for pardon is set in, Cousin Edward is no man to do things by halves. If he owned me at all, the lands would be mine again, and such a bait would be smelt out by Simon were he at the ends of the earth. Or if not, that poor child would be granted to any needy kinsman or grasping baron that Edward wanted to portion. My child shall be my own, and none other's. Better a beggar's brat than an earl's heiress!"

"She is a lovely little maiden. I know not how thou canst endure letting her grow up in poverty, an alien from her birth and rank."

"Poverty," Henry laughed. "Little knowest thou of the jolly beggar's business! I would fain wager thee, Richard, that pretty Bessee's marriage-portion shall be a heavier bag of gold than the Lady Elizabeth de Montfort would gather by all the aids due to her father from his vassals—and won moreover without curses."

"But who would be the bridegroom?"

"Her own choice, not the King's," answered Henry briefly.

"And this is all," said Richard, perceiving that according to the previous day's agreement the cream-coloured elephant of a German horse was being led forth for his use, and Sir Robert preparing to accompany him. "I must leave thee in this strange condition?"

"Ay, that must thou. Betray me, and thou shalt have the curse of the head of thine house. Had thy voice not become so strangely like my father's, I had never made myself known to thee."

"I will see thee again."

"That will be as thou canst. I trow Edward hardly gives freedom enough to his pages for them to pay visits unknown," replied Henry, with a strange sneering triumph in his own wild liberty.

"If aught ails thee, if I can aid thee, swear to me that thou wilt send to me."

Henry laughed with somewhat of a tone of mockery, adding, "Well, well—keep thou thy plight to me so long as I want thee not, and I will keep mine to thee if ever I should need thee. Now away with thee. I hear the horses impatient for thee; and what would be the lot of the beggar if he were seen chattering longer with a lordly young page than might suffice for his plaint? I hear voices. Put a tester in my dish, fair Sir, for appearance' sake. Thou hast it not? aha—I told thee I was the richer as well as the freer man. What's that? That is no ring of coin."

"'Tis a fair jewel, father, green and sparkling," cried Bessee.

"Nay, nay, I'll have none of it. Some token from thy new masters? Ha, boy?"

"From the Princess, on New Year's Day," replied Richard. "But keep it, oh, keep it, Henry; it breaks my heart to leave thee thus."

"Keep it! Not I. What wouldst say to thy dainty dame? Nor should I get half its value from the Jews. No, no, take back thy jewel, Sir Page; I'll not put thee in need of telling more lies than becomes thine office."

Richard glowed with irritation; but what was the use of anger with a blind beggar? And while Henry bestowed far more demonstration of affection on Leonillo than on his brother, it became needful to mount and ride off, resolving to tell the Prince and Princess, what would be no falsehood, that the child belonged to a Kenilworth man-at-arms, sorely wounded at Evesham, and at present befriended by the Knights of St. John.

Old Sir Robert Darcy knew so much that it was needful to confide fully in him; and he gave Richard some satisfaction by a promise to watch over his brother as far as was possible with a man of such uncertain vagrant habits; and he likewise engaged to let him know, even in the Holy Land, of any change in the beggar's condition; and this, considering the wide-spread connections of the Order, and that some of its members were sure to be in any crusading army, was all that Richard could reasonably hope.

"Canst write?" asked Sir Robert.

"Yea, Father."

"I could once! But if there be need to send thee a scroll, I'll take care it is writ by a trusty hand."

More than this Richard could not hope. There had always been a strange self-willed wildness of character about his eldest brother, who, though far less violent and overbearing in actual deed than the two next in age, Simon and Guy, had contrived to incur even greater odium than they, by his mocking careless manner and love of taunts and gibing. Simon de Montfort the elder had indeed strangely failed in the bringing up of his sons. Whether it were that their royal connection had inflated them with pride, or that the King's indulgence had counteracted the good effects of the admirable education provided for them at home, they had done little justice to their parentage, or to their tutor, the excellent Robert Grostete. Perhaps the Earl himself was too affectionate: perhaps his occupation in public affairs hindered him from enforcing family discipline. At any rate, neither of the elder three could have been naturally endowed with his largeness of mind, and high unselfish views. He was a man before his age; not only deeply pious, but with a devoted feeling for justice and mercy carried into all the details of life, till his loyalty to the law overcame his loyalty to the King. Simon and Guy, on the other hand, were commonplace young nobles of the thirteenth century, heedless of all but themselves, and disdaining all beneath them; and when their father had seized the reins of government in order to enforce the laws that the King would not observe, they saw in his elevation a means of gratifying themselves, and being above all law. The cry throughout England had been that Simon's "sons made themselves vile, and he restrained them not."

Henry de Montfort had not indeed, like his brothers, plundered the ships in the Channel, extorted money from peaceful yeomen, nor insulted the poor old captive King to his face; but his deference had been more galling than their defiance; his scornful smiles and keen cutting jests had mortally offended many a partizan; and when positive work was to be done, Simon with all his fierceness and cruelty was far more to be depended on than Henry, who might at any time fly off upon some incalculable freak. To Richard's boyish recollection, if Simon had been the most tyrannical towards him in deed, Henry had been infinitely more annoying and provoking in the lesser arts of teasing.

And looking back on the past, he could understand how intolerable a life of helplessness would be among the equals whom Henry had so often stung with his keen wit, and that to a man of his peculiar tone of mind there was infinitely more liberty in thus sinking to the lowest depths, where his infirmities were absolute capital to him, than in being hedged about with the restraints of his rank. Any way, it was impossible to interfere, even for the child's sake, and all Richard could do to console himself was to look forward to his return from the Crusade an esquire or even a knight, with exploits that Henry might respect—a standing in the Court that would give him some right to speak—perhaps in time a home and lady wife to whom his brother would intrust his child, who would then be growing out of a mere toy. Or might not his services win him a fresh grant of the earldom, and could he not then prove his sincerity by laying it at the true Earl's feet?

Pretty Bessee, too! Richard remembered stories current in the family, of their grandmother, Amicia, Countess of Leicester in her own right, being forced when a young girl to wed the stern grim old persecuting Simon de Montfort, and how vain had been her struggles against her doom. He lost himself in graceful romantic visions of the young knight whose love he would watch and foster, and whose marriage to his lovely niece should be securely concluded ere her rank should be made known, when her guardian uncle would yield all to her. And from that day forth Richard looked out with keen eyes among the playfellows of the little princes for Bessee's future knight.

CHAPTER VII—AMONG THE RUINS OF CARTHAGE

"But man is more than law, and I may have
Some impress of myself upon the world;
One poor brief life, helping to feed the flame
Of chivalry, and keep alive the truth
That courage, honour, mercy, make a knight."
Queen Isabel, by S. M.

"Land in sight! Cheer up, John, my man!" said Richard, leaning over a bundle of cloaks that lay on the deck of a Genoese galley.

The cross floated high aloft, accompanied by the lions of English royalty; the bulwark was hung round with blazoned shields, and the graceful white sails were filled by a gay breeze that sent the good ship dancing over the crested waves of the Mediterranean, in company with many another of her gallant sisters, crowded with the chivalry of England.

Woeful was however the plight of great part of that chivalry. Merrily merrily bounded the bark, but her sport felt very like death to many of her freight, and among others to poor little John de Mohun.

His father, Baron Mohun of Dunster, had been deeply implicated in the Barons' Wars, and had been a personal friend of the Earl of Leicester, from whom he had only separated himself in consequence of the outrageous exactions and acts of insolence perpetrated by the young Montforts. He had indeed received a disabling wound while fighting on the Prince's side at Evesham; but his submission had been thought so insecure that his son and heir had been required of him, ostensibly as page, but really as hostage.

In spite of his Norman surname, little John of Dunster was, at twelve years old, a sturdy thoroughgoing English lad, with the strongest possible hatred to all foreigners, whom with grand indifference to natural history he termed "locusts sucking the blood of Englishmen." Not a word or command would he understand except in his mother tongue; and no blows nor reproofs had sufficed to tame his sturdy obstinacy. The other pages had teased, fagged, and bullied him to their hearts' content, without disturbing his determination to go his own way; and his only friend and protector had been Richard, whom, under the name of Fowen, he took for a genuine Englishman, and loved with all his heart. If anything would ever cure him of his wilful awkwardness and dogged bashfulness, it was likely to be the kindness of Richard—above all, in the absence of the tormentors, for Hamlyn de Valence alone of the other pages had been selected to attend upon the Prince in this expedition; and he, though scornful and peremptory, did not think the boy worthy of his attention, and did not actively tease him.

At present Hamlyn de Valence, as well as most others of the passengers, lay prostrate; scarcely alive even to the assurance of Richard, who had still kept his feet, that the outline of the hills was quickly becoming distinct, and that they were fast entering the gulf where lay the fleet that had brought the crusaders of France and Sicily, whom they hoped to join in the conquest and conversion of Tunis. On arriving at Aigues Mortes, they had found that the French King had already sailed for Sicily; and following him thither, learnt that his brother, Charles of Anjou, had persuaded him to begin his crusade by a descent on Tunis, to which the Sicilian crown was said to have some claim; that he had sailed thither at once, and Charles had followed him so soon as the Genoese transports could return for the Sicilian troops.

"I see the masts!" exclaimed Richard; "the bay is crowded with them! There must be a goodly force. Yonder are two headlands; within them we shall have smoother water—see—"

"What strikes thee so suddenly silent?" growled one of the muffled figures stretched on deck.

"The ensigns are but half-mast high, my Lord," returned Richard in an awe-struck voice; "the lilies of France are hung drooping downward."

"These plaguy southern winds at their tricks," muttered at first Earl Gilbert of Gloucester, for he it was who had spoken, though Richard had not known him to be so near; then sitting up, he came to a fuller view: "Hm—it looks ill! Thou canst keep thy feet, Fowen, or what do they call thee? Down with thee to the cabin, and let the Prince know."

Stepping across the prostrate forms, and meeting with vituperations as he trode, Richard made his way to the ladder that led below, and notified his presence behind the curtain that veiled the royal cabin. He was summoned to enter at once. The Prince was endeavouring to write at a swinging-table, the Princess lay white and resigned on a couch, attended on by Dame Idonea (or more properly Iduna) Osbright, a lady who had lost her husband in a former Crusade, and had ever since been a sort of high-born head nurse in the palace. A Danish skald, who had once been at the English court, had said that she seemed to have eaten her namesake's apple of immortality, without her apple of beauty, for no one could ever remember to have seen her other than a tiny dried-up old witch, with keen gray eyes, a sharp tongue, an ever ready foot and hand, and a frame utterly unaffected by any of the influences so sinister to far younger and stronger ones. Devoted to all the royal family, her special passion was for Prince Edmund, who, in his mother's repugnance to his deformity, had been left almost entirely to her, and she had accompanied the Princess Eleanor all the more willingly from her desire to look after her favourite nursling.

"There, Lady," said Edward to his wife, "the tossing is all but over; here is Richard come to tell us that we are nigh on land."

"Even so, my Lord," returned Richard; "we are entering the gulf, but my Lord of Gloucester has sent me to report to you that in all the ships the colours are trailing."

"Sayst thou?" exclaimed the Prince, hastily laying aside his writing materials. "Fear not, mi Dona, I will return anon and tell thee how it is. We are in smoother water already."

"So much smoother that I will come with thee out of this stifling cabin," said Eleanor. "O would that we had been in time for thee to have counselled thine uncles—"

"We will see what we have to grieve for ere we bemoan ourselves," said the Prince. "My good uncle of France would put his whole fleet in mourning for one barefooted friar!"

"Depend on it, my Lord, 'tis mourning for something in earnest," interposed Dame Iduna; "I said it was not for nothing that a single pyot came and rocked up his ill-omened tail while we were taking horse for this expedition, and my Lady there was kissing the little ones at home, nor that a hare ran over our road at Bagshot—"

"Well, Dame," interposed the Prince good-humouredly, seeing his wife somewhat affected by the list of omens, "I know you have a horse-shoe in your luggage, so you will come safe off, whoever does not!"

"And what matters what my luck is," returned the Dame, "an old beldame such as me, so long as you and your brother come off safe, and find the blessed princes at home well and sound? Would that we were out of this sandy hole, or that any one would resolve me why we cannot go straight to Jerusalem when we are about it!"

The Dame had delayed them while she spoke, in order to adjust the Princess's muffler over her somewhat dishevelled locks; but Eleanor seeing that her husband was impatient, put a speedy end to her operations, and took his arm.

Meantime the vessel had come within the Gulf of Goletta, and others of the passengers had revived, and were standing on deck to watch their entrance into the very harbour that two thousand years before had sheltered the storm-tossed fleet of AEneas; but if the Trojan had there found a wooded haven, the groves and sylvan shades must long since have been destroyed, for to the new-comers the bay appeared inclosed by spits of sand, though there was a rising ground in front that cut off the view. In the centre of the bay was a low sandy islet, covered with remains of masonry, and with a fort in the midst. On this was mounted the French banner, but likewise drooping; and all around it lay the ships with furled sails and trailing ensigns, giving them an inexpressibly mysterious look of woe, like living creatures with folded wings and vailed crests, lying on the face of the waters in a silent sleep of sorrow. There was an awe of suspense that kept each one on the deck silent, unable to utter the conjecture that weighed upon his breast.

A boat was already putting off, and its quick movements seemed to mar the solemn stillness, as, impelled by the regular strokes of a dozen dark handsome Genoese mariners with gaily-tinted caps, it shot towards the vessel. A Genoese captain in graver garb sat at the helm, and as they came alongside, a whisper, almost a shudder, seemed to thrill upwards from the boat to the crew, and through them to the passengers, "Il Re!" "il Re santo," "il Re di Francia." It seemed to have pervaded the whole ship even before the Genoese had had time to take the rope flung to him and to climb up the ship's side, where as his fellow-captain greeted him, he asked hastily for the Principe Inglese.

For Edward had not come forward, but was standing with his back against the mainmast, with colourless cheek and eyes set and fixed. Eleanor looked up to him in silence, aware that he was mastering vehement agitation, and would endure no token of sympathy or sorrow that would unnerve him when dignity required firmness. To him, Louis IX., the husband of his mother's sister, had been the guiding friend and noble pattern denied to him in his father; and Eleanor, intrusted to his uncle's care during the troubles of England, a maiden wife in her first years of womanhood, had been formed and moulded by that holy and upright influence. To both the loss was as that of a father; and the murmur among the sailors was to them as a voice saying, "Knowest thou that God will take away thy master from thy head to-day?" For the moment, however, the Princess's sole thought was how her husband would bear it, and she watched anxiously till the struggle was over, in the space of a few seconds, and he met the Genoese with his usual reserved courtesy; and returning his salutation, signed to him to communicate his tidings.

They were however brief, for the captain had held by his ship, and all he knew was that deadly sickness, fever, and plague had raged in the camp. The Papal Legate was dead, and the good King of France. His son was dead too, and many another beside.

"Which son?"

"Not the eldest—he lay sick, but there were hopes of him; but the little one—

he had been carried on board his ship, but it had not saved him."

"Poor little Tristan!" sighed Eleanor; "true Cross-bearer, born in one hapless Crusade to die in another."

"The King of Sicily?" demanded Edward between his teeth.

"He had arrived the very day of his brother's death," said the Genoese; "and when he had seen how matters stood, he had concluded a truce with the King of Tunis, and intended to sail as soon as the new King of France could bear to be moved."

In the meantime the vessel had been anchored, and preparations were made for landing; but the Princes impatience to hear details would not brook even the delay of waiting till his horse could be set ashore. He committed to the Earl of Gloucester the charge of encamping his men on the island, left a message with him for his brother Edmund, who was in another ship, and perceiving that Richard had suffered the least of all his suite, summoned him to attend him in the boat which was at once lowered.

This would have been a welcome call had not Richard found that poor little John de Mohun had not revived like the other passengers, but still lay inert and sometimes moaning. All Richard could do was to beg the groom specially attached to the pages' service, to have a care of the little fellow, and get him sheltered in a tent as soon as possible; but the Prince never suffered any hesitation in obeying him, and it was needful to hurry at once into the boat.

Without a word, the Prince with long swift strides, in the light of the sinking sun, walked up the low hill, the same where erst the pious AEneas climbed with his faithful Achates following. From the brow the Trojan prince had beheld the rising city in the valley—the English prince came on its desolation. Yet nature had made the vale lovely—green with well-watered verdure, fields of beauteous green maize, graceful date palms, and majestic cork trees; and among them were white flat-roofed Moorish houses; but many a black stain on the fair landscape told of the fresh havoc of an invading army.

Utterly blotted out was Carthage. Half demolished, half choked with sand, the city of Dido, the city of Hannibal, the city of Cyprian— all had vanished alike, and nothing remained erect but a Moorish fortress, built up with fragments of the huge stones of the old Phoenicians, intermixed with the friezes and sculptures of Graecising Rome, and the whole fabric in the graceful Saracenic taste; while completing the strange mixture of periods, another of those mournful French banners drooped from the battlements, and around it spread the white tents of the armies of France and the Two Sicilies, like it with trailing banners; an orphaned plague-stricken host in a ruined city.

While the Prince paused for a moment's glance, a party of knights came spurring up the hill, who had been ordered off to meet him on the first intelligence that his fleet was in sight, but had been taken by surprise by his alertness.

They met with bowed heads and dejected mien; and there was one who hid his face and wept aloud as he exclaimed, "Ah! Messire, our holy King loved you well!"

"Alas, beau sire Guillaume de Porceles!" was all that Edward could say, as with tears in his eyes he held out his hand to the good Provencal knight, adding, "Let me hear!"

The knight, leading his horse and walking by Edward's side, told how the King had been induced to make his descent on Tunis, from some wild hope of the king's conversion, which had been magnified by Charles of Anjou, from his dislike to let so gallant an army pass by without endeavouring to obtain some personal advantage to his own realm of Sicily. Though a vassal of Beatrix of Provence, the Sire de Porceles was no devoted admirer of her husband, Charles of Anjou, and spoke with no concealment of the unhappy perversion of the Crusade. Charles of Anjou was all-powerful with the court of Rome, and in crusading matters Louis deemed it right absolutely to surrender to the ecclesiastical power all that judgment which had made him so prudent and wise a king at home, while his crusades were lamentable failures. Thus in him it had been a piece of obedient self-denial not to press forward to the Holy Sepulchre; but to land in this malarious bay to fulfil aims that, had he but used his common sense, he would have seen to be merely those of private ambition. There it had been one scene of wasting sickness. A few deeds of arms had been done to refresh the spirits of the French, such as the taking of the fort of Carthage, and now and then a skirmish of some foraging party; but in general the Moors launched their spears and fled without staying for combat. Many who had hid themselves in the vaults and cellars of Carthage had been dragged out and put to death, and their bodies had aided in breeding pestilence. Name after name fell from the lips of the knight, like the roll of warriors fallen in a great battle, when

"They melted from the field like snow,
Their king, their lords, their mightiest low."

And the last foreign embassy that ever reached Louis IX. had been that of the Greek Emperor Michael Palaeologos, come to set before him the savage barbarities perpetrated upon Christians by this brother -

"Who had spoilt the purpose of his life."

It was as Charles entered the port, that Louis, lying on a bed of ashes, with his hands crossed upon his breast, and the words, "O Jerusalem, Jerusalem!" entered not the Jerusalem of his earthly schemes, but the Jerusalem of his true aspirations.

"Shall we conduct you to my Lord the King of Sicily?" asked De Porceles.

"No!" said Edward, with bitter sternness; "to my uncle of France."

"Down, down, my Lord, and all of you instantly," shouted Porceles suddenly, throwing himself face downwards on the ground. Edward was too good a soldier not to follow the injunction instantaneously, and Richard did the same, as well as all the knights who had come up with Porceles. Even the horses buried their noses in the hot sandy soil. A strange rushing roaring sound passed over them; there was a sense of intense suffocation, then of heat, pricking, and irritation. The Provencals were rising; and the Prince and his page doing the same, shook off a plentiful load of sand, and beheld, careering furiously away, between them and the western sun, what looked like a purple column, reaching from earth to heaven, and bespangled with living gold-dust, whirling round in giddy spirals, and all the time fleeting so fast that it was diminishing every moment, and was gone in a wink of the eye.

"Is it enchantment?" gasped Richard to the squire nearest him, as he strove to clear his eyes from the sand and gaze after the wonder.

"Worse than enchantment," quoth the squire; "it is a sand whirlwind."

They were soon crossing the ditch that had been dug around the camp among the ruins, and passed through lanes of tents erected among the thick foliage that mantled the broken walls; here and there tracks of mosaic pavement; of temples to Dido or Anna peeping forth beneath either the luxuriant vegetation or the heavy sand-drifts; or columns of the new Carthage lying veiled by acanthus; or remnants of churches destroyed by Genseric—all alike disregarded by the sickly drooping figures that moved feebly about among them, regarding them as little save stumbling-blocks.

A Moorish house in the midst of a once well-laid-out garden, now trampled and destroyed, was the place to which the Provencal knight led the English Prince. Entering the doorway of a court, where a fountain sparkled in the midst of a marble pavement, they saw the richly-latticed stone doorway of the house guarded by two figures in armour like iron statues; and passing between them, they came into the principal chamber, marble-floored, and with a divan of cushions round it; but full in the midst of the room lay a coffin, covered with the lilied banner, and the standard of the Cross; the crowned helmet, good sword, knightly spurs, and cross-marked shield lying upon it; solemn forms in armour guarded it, and priests knelt and chanted prayers and psalms around it. Within were only the bones of Louis, which were to be taken to St. Denis. The flesh, which had been removed by being boiled in wine and spices, was already on its way to Palermo in a vessel whose melancholy ensigns would have announced the loss to the English had they not passed it in the night.

Long did Edward kneel beside the remains of his uncle, with his face hidden and thoughts beyond our power to trace. Richard's heart was full of that strange question "Wherefore?" Wherefore should the best and purest schemes planned by the highest souls fall over like a crested wave and become lost? So it had been, he would have said, with the Round Table under Arthur, so with England's rights beneath his own noble father, so with the Crusade under such leaders as Edward of England and Louis of France. Did he mark the answer in those Psalms that the priests were singing around -

"Qui seminant in lacrymis, in exultatione metent,
Euntes ibant et flebant mittentes semina sua,
Venientes autem venient cum exultatione portantes manipulos suos."
{1}

Surely we may believe that Simon of Leicester and Louis of France were alike beyond grief at their marred visions, their errors of deed or of judgment were washed away, and their true purpose was accepted, both waiting the harvest when their works should follow them, and it should have been made manifest that the effect of what they had been and had suffered had told far more on future generations than what they had wrought out in their own lifetime.

It was at that moment that the sensation that an eye was upon him caused Richard to raise his eyes from the floor. One of the armed figures, who had hitherto stood as still as suits of armour in a castle hall, had partially lowered the visor of the helmet, and eyes, nose, and a part of the cheeks were visible. Richard looked up, and they were those of his father! was it a delusion of his fancy? He closed his eyes and looked again. Again it was the deep brown Montfort eye, the clearly-cut nose, the embrowned skin! He glanced at the bearings on the shield. Behold, it was his own—the red field and white lion rampant with a forked tail, which he had not seen for so long.

Almost at the same moment another person entered the chamber—a man with a sallow complexion, narrow French features, sharp gray eyes, and a certain royal bearing that even a cunning shrewdness of expression could not destroy. His face was composed to a look of melancholy, and he crossed himself and knelt down near Edward to await the conclusion of his devotions. Edward, who knelt absorbed in grief, with his cloak partly over his face, apparently did not perceive him, and after two or three unheeded endeavours at attracting notice, he at length rose and said in a low voice, "My fair nephew." For a moment the Prince lifted up his face, and Richard had rather have died than have encountered that glance of mournful reproof; then hiding his face in his hands again, he continued his devotions.

When these were ended he rose from his knees; and when out of the death-chamber bowed his head and with grave courtesy exchanged greetings with Charles of Anjou, asking at the same time to see his young cousin Philippe, the new King of France.

An inquiry from an attendant elicited that Philippe had just dropped asleep under the influence of a potion from his leech.

"Then, fair nephew," said Charles of Sicily, "be content with your old uncle, and come to my apartments, where I will set before you the necessities that have led me to conclude the truce that is baffling your eager desire of deeds of arms."

"Pardon me, royal uncle," returned Edward, "I must see my camp set up. It is already late, and I must take order that my troops mingle not where contagion might seize them. Another time," he added, "I may brook the argument better."

Charles of Anjou did not press him further. There was that in his face and voice which betokened that his fierce indignation and overpowering grief were scarcely restrained, and that a word of excuse in his present mood would but have roused the lion.

Horses had been provided for him and his attendant. He flung himself on his steed at once, and Richard was obliged to follow without a moment's opportunity of making inquiry about the wonderful apparition he had seen in the chamber of death.

For some distance Edward galloped rapidly over the sandy soil, then drawing up his horse when he had come to the brow from which he could see on the one side the valley of Carthage, on the other the bay, he made an exclamation which Richard took for a summons, and he came up asking if he were called. "No, boy, no! I only spoke my thoughts aloud! Failure and success! We've seen them both to-day—in the two kings! What thinkst thou of them?"

"Better be wrecked than work the wreck, my Lord," said Richard.

"Ay! but why surrender the wit to the worker of the wreck?" said Edward. Then knitting his brow, "Two holy men have I known who did not blind their wit for their conscience' sake—two alone—did it fare better with them? One was the good Bishop of Lincoln—the other thou knowst, Richard! Well, one goes after another—first good Bishop Grostete, then the Lord of Leicester, and now mine uncle of France; and if earth is to have no better than such as it pleases the Saints to leave in it, it will not be worth staying in much longer."

"My Lord," said Richard, coming near, "methought I saw my father's face under a visor—one of the knightly guards beside the holy King."

"Well might thy fancy call him up in such a presence," said Edward. "They twain had hearts in the same place above, though they saw the world below on different sides, and knew each other little, and loved each other less, in life. That's all at an end now! Well, back to our camp to make the best of the world they have left behind them!" And then in a tone that Richard was not meant to hear, "While mi dona Leonor remains to me there is something saintly and softening still in this world! Heaven help me—ay, and all my foes —were she gone from it too!"

CHAPTER VIII—RICHARD'S WRAITH

"No distance breaks the tie of blood;
Brothers are brothers evermore;
Nor wrong, nor wrath of deadliest mood,
That magic may o'erpower."—Christian Year.

It was nearly dark when the Prince and the Page landed on the island, and found the tents already set up in their due order and rank, according to the discipline that no one durst transgress where Edward was the commander.

Richard attended him to his pavilion, and being there dismissed until supper-time, crossed the square space which was always left around the royal banner, to the tent at the southern corner, which was regularly appropriated to the pages' use. On lifting its curtain he was, however, dismayed to see a kirtle there, and imagining that he must have fallen upon the ladies' quarters, he was retreating with an apology; when the sharp voice of Dame Idonea called out, "Oh yes, Master Page! 'tis you that are at home here. I was merely tarrying till 'twas the will of one of you to come in and look to the poor child."

And little John of Dunster called from a couch of mantles, "Richard, oh! is it he at last?"

"It is I," said Richard, advancing into the light of a brass lamp, hung by chains from the top of the tent. "This is kind indeed, Lady! But is he indeed so ill at ease?"

"How should he be otherwise, with none of you idle-pated pages casting a thought to him?"

"I was grieved to leave him—but the Prince summoned me," began Richard.

"Beshrew thee! Tell me not of princes, as though there were no one whom thou couldst bid to have a care of the little lad!"

"I did bid Piers—," Richard made another attempt.

"Piers, quotha? Why didst not bid the Jackanapes that sits on the luggage? A proper warder for a sick babe!"

"I am no babe!" here burst out John; "I am twelve years old come Martinmas, and I need no tendance but Richard's."

"Ha, ha! So those are all the thanks we ladies get, when we are not young and fair!" laughed Dame Idonea, rather amused.

"I want no women, young or old," petulantly repeated John; "I want Richard.—Lift me up, Richard; take away this cloak."

"For his life, no!" returned the Dame; "he has the heats and the chills on him, and to let him take cold would be mere slaughter."

"Alas!" said Richard, "I hoped nothing ailed him but the sea, and that landing would make all well."

"As if the sea ever made a child shiver and burn by turns! Nay, 'tis the trick of the sun in these parts. Strange that the sun himself should be a mere ally of the Infidel! I tell thee, if the child is ever to see Dunster again, thou must watch him well, keep him from the sun by day and the chill by night; or he'll be like the poor creatures in the French camp out there, whom, I suppose, you found in fine case."

"Alack yes, Lady!"

"I've seen it many a time; and all their disorders will be creeping into our camp next. Tell me, is it even as they told us, one king dead and the other dying?"

Richard began to wonder whether he should ever get her out of his tent, for she insisted on his telling her every possible particular— who had died, who had lived, who was sick, who well; and as from the close connection between the English, French, and Sicilian courts, whose queens were all sisters, she knew who every one was, and accounted for the history of each person she inquired after, back to the last generation—happy if it were not to the third— her conversation was not quickly over. She ended at last, by desiring Richard to give her patient some of a febrifuge, which she had brought with her, every two hours, and when it was all spent, or in case of any change in the boy's state, to summon her from the ladies' tent; adding, however, "But what's the use of leaving a pert springald like thee in charge? Thou wilt sleep like a very dormouse, I'll warrant! I'd best call Mother Jugge."

"Oh no, no!" cried John; to whom the attendance of Mother Jugge would have been a worse indignity than the being nursed by Dame Idonea; "let me have no one but Richard! Richard knows all I want.—Richard, leave me not again."

"Ay, ay; a little lad ever hangs to a bigger, were he to torture the life out of him. Small thanks for us women after our good looks be past. But I'll look in on the child in early morn, thanks or no thanks; for I know his mother well, and if I can help it, the hyenas shall not make game of his bones, as I hear them doing by the French yonder."

John strove to say that, indeed, he thanked her, and had been infinitely comforted and refreshed by her care, and that all he meant was to express his distaste to Mother Jugge, the lavender (i.e. laundress), and his desire for Richard Fowen's company; but he was little attended to, and apparently more than half offended, the brisk old lady trotted away.

That island was a dreary place; without a tree or any shelter from the glare of sun and sea, whose combined influences threatened blindness, sun-stroke, or at the very least blistered the faces of those who stepped beyond their tents by day. The Prince's orders, however, strictly confined his army within its bounds, except that at twilight parties were sent ashore for water and provisions, under strict orders, however, to hold no parley with any one from the French or Sicilian camps, lest they should bring home the infection of the pestilence; and always under the command of some trustworthy knight, able and willing to enforce the command.

The Prince himself refused all participation in the counsels of Charles of Anjou, and confined himself, like his men, entirely to the fleet and island. Charles contrived to spread a report, that his displeasure was solely due to his disappointment at being balked of fighting with the Tunisians; and that instead of indignant grief at the perversion of the wrecked Crusade, he was only showing the sullenness of an aggrieved swordsman. Even young Philippe le Hardi, a dull, heavy, ignorant youth, was led to suppose this was the cause of his offence, and though daily inquiries were sent through the Genoese crews for his health, he made no demonstration of willingness to see his cousin of England.

Thus Richard had no opportunity of ascertaining whether there were any basis for the strange impression he had received in St. Louis's death-chamber. It would have been an act of disobedience, not soon overlooked by the Prince, had one of his immediate suite transgressed his commands, and indeed, so strict was the discipline, that it would scarcely have been possible to make the attempt. Besides, Richard's time was entirely engrossed between his duties in attending on the Prince, and his care of little John of Dunster, who had a sharp attack of fever, and was no doubt only carried through it by the experienced skill of Dame Idonea Osbright, and by Richard's tender nursing. Somehow the dame's heart was not won, even by the elder page's dutiful care and obedience to all her directions. Partly she viewed him as a rival in the affections of the patient—who, poor little fellow, would in his companion's absence be the child he was, and let her treat him like his mother, or old nurse, chattering to her freely about home, and his home-sick longings; whereas the instant any male companion appeared, he made it a point of honour to be the manly warrior and crusader, just succeeding so far as to be sullen instead of plaintive; though when left to Richard, he could again relax his dignity, and become natural and affectionate. But besides this species of jealousy, Richard suspected that Lady Osbright knew, or at least guessed, his own parentage, and disliked him for it accordingly. She had never forgotten the distress and degradation of his mother's stolen marriage, nor forgiven his father for it; she had often stung the proud heart of his brother Henry, when he shared the nursery of his cousins the princes; and her sturdy English dislike of foreigners, and her strong narrow personal loyalty, had alike resulted in the most vehement hatred of the Earl of Leicester, whose head she would assuredly have welcomed with barbarous exultation, worthy of her Danish ancestors. Little chance, then, was there that she would regard with favour his son under a feigned name, fostered in the Prince's own court and camp.

She was a constraint, and almost a vexation, to Richard, and he heartily wished that the boy's recovery would free his tent from her. The boy did recover favourably, in spite of all the discomforts of the island, and was decidedly convalescent when, after nearly ten days' isolation on the island, Edward drew out his whole force upon the shore to do honour to the embarkation of the relics of Louis IX. It was one of the most solemn and melancholy pageants that could be conceived. A wide lane of mailed soldiers was drawn up, Sicilians and Provencals on the one side, and on the other, English and the Knights of the two Orders. All stood, or sat on horseback in shining steel, guarding the way along which were carried the coffins. In memory, perhaps, of Louis's own words, "I, your leader, am going first," his remains headed the procession, closely followed by those of his young son; and behind it marched his two brothers, Charles and Alfonse, and his son-in-law, the King of Navarre (the two latter already bearing the seeds of the fatal malady), and the three English princes, Edward, Edmund, and Henry of Almayne, each followed by his immediate suite. The long line of coffins of French counts and nobles, whose lives had in like manner been sacrificed, brought up the rear; and alas! how many nameless dead must have been left in the ruins!

Each coffin when brought to the shore was placed in a boat, and with muffled oars transplanted to the vessel ready to receive it, while the troops remained drawn up on the shore. The procession that ensued was almost more mournful. It was still of biers, but these were not of the dead but of the living, and again the foremost was the King of France, while next to him came his sister, the Queen of Navarre. Edward went down to his litter, as it was brought on the beach, and offered him his arm as he feebly stepped forth to enter the boat. Philippe looked up to his tall cousin, and wrung his hands as he murmured, "Alas! what is to be the end of all this?" Edward made kind and cheerful reply, that things would look better when they met at Trapani, and then almost lifted the young king into his boat. Poor youth, he had not yet seen the end! He was yet to lose his wife, his brother-in-law, and his uncle and aunt, ere he should see his home again.

Richard and Hamlyn de Valence, as part of the Prince's train, had moved in the procession; and they were for the rest of the day in close attendance on their lord, conveying his numerous orders for the embarkation of the troops on the morrow, on their return to Sicily. It was not till night-fall that Richard returned to his tent, where John of Dunster was sitting on the sand at the door, eagerly watching for him. "Well, Jack, my lad, how hast thou sped?" asked he, advancing. "Couldst see our doleful array?"

"Is it thou, indeed, this time?" said the boy, catching at his cloak.

"Why, who should it be?"

"Thy wraith! Thy double-ganger has been here Richard."

"What, dreaming again?"

'No no! I am well, I am strong. But this IS the land of enchantment! Thou knowst it is. Did we not see a fleet of fairy boats sailing on the sea? and a leaf eat up a fly here on this very tent pole? And did not the Fay Morgaine show us towns and castles and churches in the sea? Thou didst not call me light-headed then, Richard; thou sawest it too!"

"But this wraith of mine! Where didst see it?"

"In this tent. I was lying on the sand, trying if I could make it hold enough to build a castle of it, when the curtain was put back, and there thou stoodest, Richard!"

"Well, did I speak or vanish?"

"Oh, thou spakest—I mean the THING spake, and it said, 'Is this the tent of the young Lord of Montfort?' How now—what have I said?"

"Whom did he ask for?" demanded Richard breathlessly.

"Montfort—young Lord de Montfort!" replied John; "I know it was, for he said it twice over."

"And what didst thou answer?"

"What should I answer? I said we had no Montforts here; for they were all dishonoured traitors, slain and outlawed."

Richard could not restrain a sudden indignant exclamation that startled the boy. "Every one says so! My father says so!" he returned, somewhat defiantly.

"Not of the Earl," said Richard, recollecting himself.

"He said every one of the young Montforts was a foul traitor, and man-sworn tyrant, as bad as King John had been ere the Charter," repeated John hotly, "and their father was as bad, since he would give no redress. Thou knowst how they served us in Somerset and Devon!"

"I have heard, I have heard," said Richard, cutting short the story, and controlling his own burning pain, glad that the darkness concealed his face. "No more of that; but tell me, what said this stranger?"

"Thou thinkest it was really a stranger, and not thy wraith?" said John anxiously. "I hope it was, for Dame Idonea said if it were a wraith, it betokened that thou wouldst not—live long—and oh, Richard! I could not spare thee!"

And the little fellow came nestling up to his friend's breast in an access of tenderness, such as perhaps he would have disdained save in the darkness.

"Did Dame Idonea see him?" asked Richard. "No;

but she came in soon after he had vanished."

"Vanished! What, like Fay Morgaine's castles? Tell me in sooth, John; it imports me to know. What did this stranger, when thou spakest thus of the House of Montfort?"

"He answered," said John; "he did not answer courteously—he said, that I was a malapert little ass, and demanded again where this young Montfort's tent was. So then I said, that if a Montfort dared to show his traitor's face in this camp, the Prince would hang him as high as Judas; for I wanted to be rid of him, Richard! it was so dreadful to see thy face, and hear thy voice talking French, and asking for dead traitors."

"French!" said Richard. "Methought thou knewst no French!"

"I—I have heard it long now, more's the pity," faltered John, "and— and I'd have spoken anything to be rid of that shape."

"And wert thou rid? What befell then?"

"It cursed the Prince, and King, and all of them," said John with a shudder; "it looked black and deadly, and I crossed myself, and said the Blessed Name, and no doubt it writhed itself and went off in brimstone and smoke, for I shut my eyes, and when I looked up again it was gone!"

"Gone! Didst look after him?"

"Oh, no! Earthly things are all food for a brave man's sword," said Master John, drawing himself up very valiantly, "but wraiths and things from beneath —they do scare the very heart out of a man. And I lay, I don't know how, till Dame Idonea came in; and she said either the foul fiend had put on thy shape because he boded thee ill, or it was one of the traitor brood looking for his like."

"Tell me, John," said Richard anxiously; "surely he was not in all points like me. Had he our English white cross?"

"I cannot say as to the cross," said John; "meseemed it was all you— yourself —and that was all—only I thought your voice was strange and hollow—and —now I think of it—yes—he was bearded—brown bearded. And," with a sudden thought, "stand up, prithee, in the opening of the tent;" and then taking his post where he had been sitting at the time of the apparition, "He was not so tall as thou art. Thy head comes above the fold of the curtain, and his, I know, did not touch it, for I saw the light over it. Then thou dost not think it was thy wraith?" he added anxiously.

"I think my wraith would have measured me more exactly both in stature and in age," said Richard lightly. "But how did Leonillo comport himself? He brooks not a stranger in general; and dogs cannot endure the presence of a spirit."

"Ah! but he fawned upon this one, and thrust his nose into his hand," said John, "and I think he must have run after him; for it was so long ere he came back to me, that I had feared greatly he was gone, and oh, Richard! then I must have gone too! I could never have met you without Leonillo."

By this time Richard had little doubt that the visitor must have been one of his brothers, Simon or Guy, who were not unlikely to be among the Provencals, in the army of Charles of Anjou. He had not been thought to resemble them as a boy, but he had observed how much more alike brothers appear to strangers than they do to their own family; and he knew by occasional observations from the Prince, as well as from his brother Henry's recognition of his voice, that the old Montfort characteristics must be strong in himself. He would not, however, avow his belief to John of Dunster. Secrecy on his own birth had been enjoined on him by his uncle the King; and disobedience to the old man's most trifling commands was always sharply resented by the Prince; nor was the boy's view of the House of Montfort very favourable to such a declaration. Richard really loved the brave little fellow, and trusted that some day when the discovery must be made, it would be coupled with some exploit that would show it was no name to be ashamed of. So he only told the boy that he had no doubt the stranger was a foreign knight, who had once known the old Leicester family; but bade him mention the circumstance to no one. He feared, however, that the caution came too late, since Dame Idonea was not only an inveterate gossip, but was likely to hold in direful suspicion any one who had been inquired for by such a name.

The personal disappointment of having missed his brother was great. Richard was very lonely. The Princes, and Hamlyn de Valence, were the only persons who knew his secret, and both by Prince Edmund and De Valence he was treated with indifference or dislike. Edward himself, though the object of his fervent affection, and his protector in all essentials, was of a reserved nature, and kept all his attendants at a great distance. On very rare occasions, when his feelings had been strongly stirred—as in the instance of his visit to his uncle's death-chamber—he might sometimes unbend; and momentary flashes from the glow of his warm deep heart went further in securing the love and devotion of those around him, than would the daily affability of a lower nature; but in ordinary life, towards all concerned with him except his nearest relations, he was a strict, cold, grave disciplinarian, ever just, though on the side of severity, and stern towards the slightest neglect or breach of observance, nor did he make any exception in favour of Richard. If the youth seldom received one of his brief annihilating reproofs, it was because they were scarcely ever merited; but he had experienced that any want of exactitude in his duties was quite as severely visited as if he had not been the Prince's close kinsman, romantically rescued by him, and placed near his person by his special desire. And Eleanor, with all her gentle courtesy and kindness, was strictly withheld by her husband from pampering or cockering his pages; nor did she ever transgress his will.

The atmosphere was perhaps bracing, but it was bleak: and there were times when Richard regretted his acceptance of the Prince's offer, and yearned after family ties, equality, and freedom. Simon and Guy had never been kind to him, but at least they were his brothers, and with them disguise and constraint would be over—he should, too, be in communication with his mother and sister. He was strongly inclined to cast in his lot with them, and end this life of secrecy, and distrust from all around him save one, and his loyal love ill requited even by that one. It grieved him keenly that one of his brothers should have been repulsed from his tent; an absolutely famished longing for fraternal intercourse gained possession of him, and as he lay on his pallet that night in the dark, he even shed tears at the thought of the greeting and embrace that he had missed.

Still he had hopes for the future. There must be meetings and possibilities of inquiries passing between the three armies, and he would let no opportunity go by. The next day, however, there was no chance. The English troops were embarked in their vessels, and after a short and prosperous passage were again landed at Trapani, the western angle of Sicily. The French had sailed first, but were not in harbour when the English came in; and the Sicilians, who had brought up the rear, arrived the next day, but still there was no tidings of the French. Towards the evening, however, the royal vessel bearing Philippe III. came into harbour, and all the rest were in sight, when at sunset a frightful storm arose, and the ships were in fearful case. Many foundered, many were wrecked on the rocky islets around the port, and the French army was almost as much reduced in numbers as it had been by the Plague of Carthage.

Charles of Anjou remained himself in the town of Trapani, but knowing the evils of crowding a small space with troops, he at once sent his men inland, and Richard was again disappointed of the hope of seeing or hearing of his brothers; for the Prince still forbade all intercourse with the shattered remnant of the French army, justly dreading that they might still carry about them the seeds of the infection of the camp.

The three heads of the Crusade, however, met in the Castle of Trapani to hold council on their future proceedings. The place was the state-chamber of the castle.

Each prince had brought with him a single attendant, and the three stood in waiting near the door, in full view of their lords, though out of earshot. It was an opportunity that Richard could not bear to miss of asking for his brothers, unheard by any of those English ears who would be suspicious about his solicitude for the House of Montfort. A lively-looking Neapolitan lad was the attendant of King Charles; and in spite of all the perils of attempting conversation while thus waiting, Richard had—while the princes were greeting one another, and taking their seats—ventured the question, whether any of the sons of the English Earl of Leicester were in the Sicilian army. Of Earl of Leicester the Italian knew nothing; but Count of Montfort was a more familiar sound. "Si, si, vero!" Sicily had rung with it; and Count Rosso Aldobrandini, of the Maremma Toscana, had given his only daughter and heiress to the banished English knight, Guido di Monforte, who had served in the king's army as a Provencal.

Richard's heart beat high. Guy a well-endowed count, with a castle, lands, and home! He would have asked where Guy now was, and how far off was the Maremma; but the conference between the princes was actually commencing, and silence became necessary on the part of their attendants.

They could only hear the murmur of voices; but could discern plainly the keen looks and animated gestures of Charles of Anjou, the sickly sullen indifference of Philippe, and the majestic gravity of Edward, whose noble head towered above the other two as if he were their natural judge. Charles was, in fact, trying to persuade the others to sail with him for Greece, and there turn their forces on the unfortunate Michael Palaeologos, who had lately recovered Constantinople, the Empire that Charles hoped to win for himself, the favoured champion of Rome.

Philippe merely replied that he had had enough of crusading, he was sick and weary, he must go home and bury his father, and get himself crowned. Charles might be then seen trying a little hypocrisy; and telling Philippe that his saintly father would only have wished to speed him on the way of the Cross. Then that trumpet voice of Edward, whose tones Richard never missed, answered, "What is the way of the Cross, fair uncle?"

It was well known that Louis IX. had refused to crusade against Christians, even Greek Christians, and Philippe soon sheltered himself under the plea that had not at first occurred to his dull mind. In effect, he laid particulars before his uncle, that quickly made it plain that the French army was in too miserable a condition to do anything but return home; and Charles then addressed his persuasions to Edward—striving to convince him in the first place of the sanctity of a war against Greek heretics, and when Edward proved past being persuaded that arms meant for the recovery of the Holy Sepulchre ought not to be employed against Christians who reverenced it, he tried to demonstrate the uselessness of hoping to conquer the Holy Land, even by such a Crusade as had been at first planned, far less with the few attached to Edward's individual banner. Long did the king argue on. His low voice was scarcely audible, even without the words; but Edward's brief, ringing, almost scornful, replies, never failed to reach Richard's ear, and the last of them was, "It skills not, my fair uncle. For the Holy Land I am vowed to fight, and thither would I go had I none with me but Fowen, my groom!"

And withal his eye lit on Richard, with a look of certainty of response; of security that here was one to partake his genuine ardour, and of refreshment in the midst of his disgust with the selfish uncle and sluggish cousin. That look, that half smile, made the youth's heart bound once more. Yes, with him he would go to the ends of the earth! What was the freedom of Guy's castle, to the following of such a lord and leader in such a cause?

Richard could have thrown himself at his feet, and poured forth pledges of fidelity. But in ten minutes he was following home the unapproachable, silent, cold warrior.

And the lack of any outlet for his aspirations turned them back upon themselves, with a strange sense of bitterness and almost of resentment. Leonillo alone, as the creature lay at his feet, and looked up into his face with eyes of deep wistful meaning, seemed to him to have any feeling for him; and Leonillo became the recipient of many an outpouring of something between discontent and melancholy. Leonillo, the sole remnant of his home! He burnt for that Holy Land where he was to win the name and fame lacking to him; but there was to be long delay.

Fain would the Prince have proceeded at once to Palestine; but the Genoese, from whom, in the abeyance of the English navy, he had been obliged to hire his transports, absolutely refused to sail for the East until after the three winter months; and he was therefore obliged to remain in Sicily. King Charles invited him to spend Christmas at the court at Syracuse or Naples, in hopes, perhaps, of persuading him to the Greek expedition; but Edward was far too much displeased with the Angevin to accept his hospitality; recollecting, perhaps, that such a sojourn had been little beneficial to his great- uncle Coeur de Lion's army. He decided upon staying where he was, in the remotest corner of Sicily, and keeping his three hundred crusaders as much to themselves and to strict military discipline as possible, maintaining them at his own cost, and avoiding as far as he could all transactions with the cruel and violent Provencal adventurers, with whom Charles had filled the island.

Thus Richard found his hopes of obtaining further intelligence about his brothers entirely passing away. He did, indeed, venture on one day saying to the Prince, "My Lord, I hear that my brother Guy hath become a Neapolitan count!"

"A Tuscan robber would be nearer the mark!" coldly replied Edward.

"And," added Richard, "methought, while the host is in winter quarters, I would venture on craving your license, my Lord, to visit him?"

"Thou hast thy choice, Richard," answered the Prince, with grave displeasure; "loyalty and honour with me, or lawlessness and violence with thy brother. Both cannot be thine!"

And returning to his study of the Lais of Marie de France, he made it evident that he would hear no more, and left Richard to a sharp struggle; in which hot irritation and wounded feeling would have carried him away at once from the stern superior who required the sacrifice of all his family, and gave not a word of sympathy in return. It was the crusading vow alone that detained the youth. He could not throw away his pledge to the wars of the Cross, and it was plain that if he went now to seek out Guy, he should never be allowed to return to the crusading army. But that vow once fulfilled, proud Edward should see, that not merely sufferance but friendliness was needed to bind the son of his father's sister to his service. The brother at Bednall Green was right, this bondage was worse than beggary. Nor, under the influence of these feelings, had Richard's service the alacrity and affection for which it had once been remarkable: the Prince rebuked his short-comings unsparingly, and thus added to the sense of injury that had caused them; Hamlyn de Valence sneered, and Dame Idonea took good care to point out both the youth's neglects and his sullenness, and to whisper significantly that she did not wonder, considering the stock he came of. A soothing word or gentle excuse from the kind-hearted Princess were the only gleams of comfort that rendered the present state of things endurable.

Just after Christmas arrived a vessel with reinforcements from home. Among them came a small body of Hospitaliers, with the novice Raynal at their head, now a full-blown knight, in dazzling scarlet and white, as Sir Reginald Ferrers. Richard at once recognized him, when he came to present himself to the Prince, and was very desirous of learning whether he knew aught of that other brother, so mysteriously hidden in obscurity. Sir Raynal on his side seemed to share the desire; he exchanged a friendly glance with the page, and when the formality of the reception was over sought him out, saying, "I have a greeting for you, Master Fowen."

"From Sir Robert Darcy?" asked Richard. "How fares it with the kind old knight?"

"Excellent well! Nay, nothing fares amiss with Father Robert!" said the young knight, smiling. "Everything is the very best that could have befallen him—to hear him speak. He is the very sunshine of the Spital, and had he been ordered on this Crusade, I think all the hamlets round would have risen to withhold him."

"Ah!" said Richard, hoping he was acting indifference; "said he aught of the little maiden with the blind father?"

"Pretty Bessee and Blind Hal of Bednall Green? Verily, that was the purport of my message. The poor knave hath been sorely sick and more cracked than ever this autumn; insomuch that Father Robert spent whole nights with him; and though he be better now, and as much in his senses as e'er he will be, such another access is like to make an end of him. Now, Father Robert saith that you, Sir Page, know who the poor man is by birth, and that he prays you to send him word what had best be done with the child, in case either of his death or of his getting so frenzied as to be unable to take care of her."

"Send him word!" repeated Richard in perplexity.

"We shall certainly have some one returning soon to the Spital," replied Sir Raynal. "Indeed, methinks some of the princes will be like to return, for the old King of the Romans is failing fast, and King Henry implored that the Prince of Almayne would come to hearten him."

"Then must I write to Sir Robert?" said Richard; "mine is scarce a message for word of mouth."

"So he said it was like to be," returned the knight, "and he took thought to send you a slip of parchment, knowing, he said, that such things are not wont to be found in a crusader's budget. Moreover, if ink be wanting, he bade me tell you that there's a fish in these seas, with many arms, and very like the foul fiend, that carries a bag of ink as good as any scrivener s.

"I have seen the monster," said Richard, who had often been down to the beach to see the unlading of the fishermen's boats, and to share little John of Dunster's unfailing marvel, that the Mediterranean should produce such outlandish creatures, so alien to his Bristol Channel experiences.

And the very next time the boats came in, Richard made his way to the shore, on the beautiful, rocky, broken coast; and presently encountered a sepia, which fully justified Sir Robert's comparison, lying at the bottom of a boat. The fisherman intended it for his own dinner, when all his choicer fish should have gone to supply the Friday's meal of the English chivalry; and he was a good deal amazed when the young gentlemàn, making his Provencal as like Sicilian as he could, began to traffic with him for it, and at last made him understand that it was only its ink-bag that he wanted.

The said ink, secured in a shell, was brought home by Richard, together with a couple of the largest sea-bird's quills that he could find—and which he shaped with his dagger, as best he might, in remembrance of Father Adam de Marisco's writing lessons. He meditated what should be the language of his letter, which was not likely to be secure from the eyes of the few who could read it; and finally decided that English was the tongue known to the fewest readers, who, if they knew letters at all, were sure to be acquainted with French and Latin.

On a strip of parchment, then, about nine inches long and three wide, he proceeded to indite, in upright cramped letters, with many contractions, nearly in such terms as these -

REVEREND AND KNIGHTLY FATHER,

The good ghostly father and knight, Sir Raynald Ferrers, hath borne to me your tidings of my brother's sickness, and of all your goodness to him— whereof I pray that our blessed Lady and good St. John may reward you, for I can only pray for you. Touching his poor little daughter, in case of his death or frenzy, which the Saints of their mercy forefend, I would entreat you of your goodness to place her in some nunnery, but without making known her name and quality until my return; so Heaven bring me home safe. But an if I should be slain in this Eastern land, then were it most for the little one's good to present her to the gracious lady Princess, by whom she would be most lovingly and naturally cared for; and would be more safe than with such as might shun to own her rights of blood and heirship. Commend me to my brother, if so be that he cares to hear of me; and tell him that Guy hath wedded the lady of a castle in the land of Italy. And so praying you, ghostly father, for your blessing, I greet you well, and rest your grateful bedesman and servant,

RICHARD OF LEICESTER.

Given at the Prince's camp at Drepanum, in the realm of Sicilia, on the octave of the Epiphany, in the year of grace MCCLXX.; and so our Lord have you heartily in His keeping.

Letter-writing was a mighty task; and Richard's extemporary implements were not of the best. He laboured hard over his composition, kneeling against a chest in the tent. When at length he raised his head, he encountered a face full of the most utter amazement. Little John of Dunster had come into the tent, and stood gazing at him with open eyes and gaping mouth, as if he were perpetrating an incantation. Richard could not help laughing.

"Why, Jack, dost think I am framing a spell for thee?"

"Writing!" gasped John, relieving his distended mouth by at length closing it.

"Wherefore not? Did not I see the chaplain teaching thee to write at Guildford?"

"Ay—but that was when I was a babe! Writing! Why, my father never writes!"

"But the Prince does. Thou hast seen him write. Come now," added Richard: "if thou wilt, I will help thee to write a letter to send thy greetings home to Dunster. Thy father and mother will be right glad to hear thou hast 'scaped that African fever."

"They!—They'd think me no better than a French monk!" said John. "And none of them could read it either! I'll never write! My grandsire only set his cross to the great charter!"

And John retreated—in fear perhaps that Richard would sully his manhood with a writing lesson!

The letter was rolled up in a scroll, bound with a silken thread, and committed to the charge of Sir Raynald Ferrers, who was going shortly to be commandery of his Order at Castel San Giovanni, whence he had no doubt of being able to send the letter safely to Sir Robert Darcy, at the Grand Priory.

It would perhaps have been more expeditious to have intrusted the letter to one of the suite of Prince Henry of Almayne, who had been recalled by the tidings of the state of his father's health; but Richard dreaded betraying his brother's secret too much to venture on confiding the missive to any of this party—none of whom were indeed likely to wish to oblige him. Hamlyn de Valence was going with Henry as his esquire; and his absence seemed to Richard like the beginning of better days.

CHAPTER IX—ASH WEDNESDAY

"Mostrocci un ombra da l' un canto sola
Dicendo 'Colui feese in grembo a Dio
Lo cuor che'n su Tamigi ancor si cola.'"
DANTE. Inferno.

Shrovetide had come, and the Prince had, before leaving Trapani, been taking some share in the entertainments of the Carnival. Personally, his grave reserve made gaieties distasteful to him; and the disastrous commencement of the Crusade weighed on his spirits. But when state and show were necessary, he provided for them with royal bounty and magnificence, and caused them to be regulated with the admirable taste of that age of exceeding beauty in which he lived.

Thus, in this festal season, banquets were provided, and military shows took place, for the benefit of the Sicilian nobility and of the citizens of Trapani, on such a scale, that the English rose high in general esteem; and many were the secret wishes that Edmund of Lancaster rather than Charles of Anjou had been able to make good the grant from the Pope.

Splendid were the displays, and no slight toil did they involve on the part of the immediate train of the Prince, few in number as they were, and destitute of the appliances of the resident court. Richard hurrying hither and thither, and waiting upon every one, had little of the diversion of the affair; but he would willingly have taken treble the care and toil in the relief it was to be free from the prying mistrustful eyes of Hamlyn de Valence. Looking after little John of Dunster was, however, no small part of his trouble; the urchin was so certain to get into some mischief if left to himself— now treading on a lady's train, now upsetting a flagon of wine, now nearly impaling himself upon the point of a whole spitful of ortolans that were being handed round to the company, now becoming uncivilly deaf upon his French ear. Altogether, it was a relief to Richard's mind when he stumbled upon the little fellow fast asleep, even though it was in the middle of the Princess's violet velvet and ermine mantle, which she had laid down in order to tread a stately measure with Sire Guillaume de Porceles.

After all Richard's exertions that evening, it was no wonder that the morning found him fast asleep at the unexampled hour of eight! His wakening was a strange one. His little fellow-page was standing beside him with a strange frightened yet important air.

"What is the matter, John? It is late? Is the Prince gone to Mass? Has he missed me?" cried Richard, starting up in dismay, for unpunctuality was a great offence with Edward.

"He is gone to Mass," said John, "but, before he comes back," he came near and lowered his voice, "Hob Longbow sent me to say you had better flee."

"Flee! Boy, why should I flee? Are YOUR senses fleeing?"

"O Richard," cried John, his face clearing up, "then it is not true! You are not one of the traitor Montforts!"

"If I were a hundred Montforts, what has that to do with it?"

"Then all is well," exclaimed the boy. "I said you were no such thing! I'll tell Hob he lied in his throat."

"If he said I was a traitor, verily he did; but as to being a Montfort—But, how now, John, what means all this?"

"Then it is so! O Richard, Richard, you cannot be one of them! You cannot have written that letter to warn them to murder Prince Henry."

"To murder Prince Henry!" Richard stood transfixed. "Not the Prince's little son!"

"Oh no, Prince Henry of Almayne! At Viterbo! Hamlyn de Valence saw it. He is come back. It was in the Cathedral. O Richard—at the elevation of the Host! Guy and Simon de Montfort fell on him, stabbed him to the heart, and rushed out. Then they came back again, and dragged him by the hair of his head into the mire, and shouted that so their father had been dragged through the streets of Evesham. And then they went off to the Maremma! And," continued the boy breathlessly, "Hob Long-bow is on guard, and he bade me tell you, that for love of your father he will let you pass; and then you can hide; if only you can go ere the Prince comes forth."

"Hide! Wherefore should I hide? This is most horrible, but it is no deed of mine!" said Richard. "Who dares to think it is?"

"Then you are none of them! You had no part in it! I shall tell Hob he is a villain—"

"Stay," said Richard, laying a detaining hand on the boy. "Why does Hob think me in danger? Is anything stirring against me?"

"They all—all of poor Prince Henry's meine, that are come back with Hamlyn —say that you are a Montfort too, and—oh! do not look so fierce!—that you sent a letter to warn your brethren where to meet, and fall on the Prince. And the murderers being fled, they are keen to have your life; and, Richard, you know I saw you write the letter."

"That you saw me write a letter, is as certain as that my name is Montfort," said Richard, "but I am not therefore leagued with traitors or murderers! In the church, saidst thou? Oh, well that the Prince forbade me to visit Guy!"

"Then you will not flee?"

"No, forsooth. I will stay and prove my innocence."

"But you are a Montfort! And I saw you write the letter."

"Did you speak of my having written the letter?" asked Richard, pausing.

The boy hung his head, and muttered something about Dame Idonea.

By this time, even if Richard had thought of flight, it would have been impossible. Two archers made their presence apparent at the entrance of the tent, and in brief gruff tones informed Richard that the Prince required his presence. The space between his tent and the royal pavilion was short, but in those few steps Richard had time to glance over the dangers of his position, and take up his resolution though with a certain stunned sense that nothing could be before the member of a proscribed family, but failure, suspicion, and ruin.

The two brothers, Edward and Edmund, with the Earl of Gloucester, and their other chief councillors, were assembled; and there were looks of deep concern on the faces of all, making Edward's more than ever like a rigid marble statue; while Edmund had evidently been weeping bitterly, though his features were full of fierce indignation. Hamlyn de Valence, and a few other members of the murdered Prince's suite, stood near in deep mourning suits.

"Richard de Montfort," said Prince Edward, looking at him with a sorrowful reproachful sternness that went to his heart, "we have sent for you to answer for yourself, on a grave charge. You have heard of that which has befallen?"

"I have heard, my Lord, of a foul crime which my soul abhors. I trust none present here think me capable of sharing in it! Whoever dares to accuse me, shall be answered by my sword!" and he glanced fiercely at Hamlyn.

"Hold!" said Edward severely, "no one is so senseless as to accuse you of taking actual part in a crime that took place beyond the sea; but there is only too much reason to believe that you have been tampered with by your brothers."

Then, as his brother Edmund made some suggestion to him, he added, "Is John de Mohun of Dunster here?"

"Yea, my Lord," said the little boy, coming forward, with a flush on his face, and a bold though wistful look, "but verily Richard is no traitor, be he who he may!"

"That is not what we wished to ask of you," said the Prince, too sad and earnest to be amused even for a moment. "Tell us whom you said, even now, you had seen in the tent you shared with him in Africa."

"I said I had seen his wraith," said John.

No smile lighted upon the Prince's features; they were as serious as those of the boy, as he commented, "His likeness—his exact likeness- -you mean."

"Ay," said the boy; "but Richard proved to me after, that it had been less tall, and was bearded likewise. So I hoped it did not bode him ill."

"Worse, I fear, than if it had in sooth been his double," said Gloucester to Prince Edmund. The Prince added the question whether this visitor had spoken; and John related the inquiry for Richard by the name of Montfort, and his own reply, which elicited a murmur of amused applause among the bystanders.

The Prince, however, continued in the same grave manner to draw from the little witness his account of Richard's injunction to secresy; and then asked about the letter-writing, of which John gave his plain account. The Prince then said, "Speak now, Hamlyn."

"This, then, I have to add, my Lord, that I, as all the world, remarked that Richard de Montfort consorted much with Sir Reginald de Ferrieres, who, as we all remember, is the son of a family deeply concerned in the Mad Parliament. By Sir Reginald, on his arrival at Castel San Giovanni, a messenger is despatched, bearing letters to the Hospital at Florence, and it is immediately after his arrival there, that the two Montforts speed from the Maremma to the unhappy and bloody Mass at Viterbo."

You hear, Richard!" said the Prince. "I bade you choose between me and your brothers. Had you believed me that you could not serve both, it had been better for you. I credit not that you incited them to the assassination; but your tidings led them to perpetrate it. I cannot retain the spy of the Montforts in my camp."

"My Lord," said Richard, at last finding space for speech, "I deny all collusion with my brothers. I have neither seen, spoken with, nor sent to them by letter nor word."

"Then to whom was this letter?" demanded the Prince.

"To Sir Robert Darcy, the Grand Prior of England," answered Richard.

A murmur of incredulous amazement was heard.

"The purport?" continued Edward.

"That, my Lord, it consorts not with my duty to tell."

"Look here, Richard," interposed Gilbert of Gloucester, "this is an unlikely tale. You can have no cause for secrecy, save in connection with these brothers; and if you will point to some way of clearing yourself of being art and part in this foul act of murder, you may be sent scot free from the camp; but if you wilfully maintain this denial, what can we do but treat you as a traitor? No obstinacy! What can a lad like you have to say to good old Sir Robert Darcy, that all the world might not know?"

"My Lord of Gloucester," said Richard, "I am bound in honour not to reveal the matters between me and Sir Robert; I can only declare on the faith of a Christian gentleman that I have neither had, nor attempted to have, any dealings with either of my brothers, Guy or Simon; and if any man says I have, I will prove his falsehood on his body." And Richard flung down his glove before the Prince.

At the same moment Hamlyn de Valence sprang forward.

"Then, Richard de Montfort, I take up the gage. I give thee the lie in thy throat, and will prove on thy body that thou art a man-sworn traitor, in league with thy false brethren."

"I commit me to the judgment of God," said Richard, looking upwards.

"My Lord," said Hamlyn, "have we your permission to fight out the matter?"

"You have," said Edward, "since to that holy judgment Richard hath appealed."

But the Prince looked far from contented with the appeal. He allowed the preliminaries of place and time to be fixed without his interposition; and when the council broke up, he fixed his clear deep eyes upon Richard in a manner which seemed to the boy to upbraid him with the want of confidence, for which, however, he would not condescend to ask. Richard felt that, let the issue of the combat be what it would, he had lost that full trust on the part of the Prince, which had hitherto been his one drop of comfort; and if he were dismissed from the camp, he should be more than ever desolate, for his soul could scarce yet bring itself to grasp the horror of the crime of his brothers.

The combat could not take place for two days—waiting, on one, in order that Hamlyn might have time to rest, and recover his full strength after his voyage, and the next, because it was Ash Wednesday. In the meantime Richard was left solitary; under no restraint, but universally avoided. The judicial combat did not make him uneasy; the two youths had often measured their strength together, and though Hamlyn was the elder, Richard was the taller, and had inherited something of the Plantagenet frame, so remarkable in those two

Lords of the biting axe and beamy spear,

"wide conquering Edward" and "Lion Richard"; and each believed in the righteousness of his own cause sufficiently to have implicit confidence that the right would be shown on his side.

In fact, Richard soon understood that though Prince Edward, with a sense of the value of definite evidence far in advance of the time, and befitting the English Justinian, had only allowed the charge to be brought against him which could in a manner be substantiated, yet that the general belief went much further. Proved to be a Montfort, and to have written a letter, he was therefore convicted, by universal consent, of a league with his brothers for the revenge of their house; to have instigated the assassination at Viterbo, and to be only biding his time for the like act at Trapani. Even the Prince was deeply offended by his silence, and imputed it to no good motive; trust and affection were gone, and Richard felt no tie to retain him where he was, save his duty as a crusader. Let him fail in the combat, and the best he could look for would be to be ignominiously branded and expelled: let him gain, and he much doubted whether, though the ordeal of battle was always respected, he would regain his former position. With keen suffering and indignation, he rebelled against Edward's harshness and distrust. He—who had brought him there— who ought to have known him better! Moreover, there was the crushing sense of the guilt of his brothers; guilt most horrible in its sacrilegious audacity, and doubly shocking to the feelings of a family where the grim sanctity of the first Simon de Montfort, and the enlightened devotion of the second, formed such a contrast to the savage outrage of him who now bore their name. Richard, as with bare feet and ashes whitening his dark locks he knelt on the cold stones of the dark Norman church at Trapani, wept hot and bitter tears of humiliation over the family crimes that had brought them so low; prayed in an agony for repentance for his brothers; and for himself, some opening for expiating their sin against at least the generous royal family. "O! could I but die for my Prince, and know that he forgave and they repented!"

Only when on his way back to the camp was he sensible of the murmurs of censure at his hypocrisy in joining the penitential procession at all. Dame Idonea, in a complete suit of sackcloth, was informing her friends that she had made a vow not to wash her face till the whole adder brood of Montfort had been crushed; and that she trusted to see the beginning of justice done to-morrow. She had offered a candle to St. James to that effect, hoping to induce him to turn away his patronage from the family.

Every one, knight or squire, shrank away from Richard, if he did but look towards them; and he was seriously discomfited by the difficulty of obtaining a godfather for the combat. No one chose even to be asked, lest they might be suspected of approving of the murder of Prince Henry; and the unhappy page re-entered his tent with the most desolate sense of being abandoned by heaven and man.

Fastened upon the pole of the tent by an arrowhead, a small scroll of parchment met his eyes. He read in English—"A steed and a lance are ready for the lioncel who would rather avenge his father than lick the tyrant's feet. A guide awaits thee."

Some weeks since, this might have been a tempting summons; but now the sickening sense of the sacrilegious murder, and of the life of outlawry utterly unrestrained, passed over Richard. Yet, if he should not accept the offer, what was before him? A shameful death, perhaps; if he failed in the ordeal, disgrace, captivity, or expulsion; if he succeeded, bondage and distrust for ever. Some new accusation! some deeper fall!

There was a low growl from Leonillo; the hangings of the tent were raised, and an archer bending his head said, "A word with you, Sir."

"Who art thou?" demanded Richard.

"Hob Longbow, Sir. Remember you not old passages—in the forest, there—and Master Adam?"

Richard did remember the archer in the days of his outlaw life, in a very different capacity.

"You were grown so tall, Sir, and so hand and glove with the Longshanks, that Nick Dustifoot and I knew not an if it were yourself—but now your name is out, and the wind is in another quarter"—he grinned, then seeing Richard impatient of the approach to familiarity, "You did not know Nick Dustifoot? He was one of young Sir Simon's men-at-arms, you see, and took to the woods, like other folk, after Kenilworth was given up, till stout men were awanting for this Crusade. And he knew Sir Guy when he came to the camp yon by Tunis, and spake with him; moreover, he went in the train of him of Almayne to Viterbo, and had speech again with Sir Simon, who gave him this scroll. And if you will meet him at the Syren's Rock to-night, my Lord Richard, he will bring you to those who will conduct you to Sir Guy's brave castle, where he laughs kings and counts to scorn! We have the guard, and will see you safe past the gates of the camp."

The way to liberty was open: Richard deliberated. The atmosphere of distrust and suspicion under the Prince's coldness was well-nigh unbearable. Danger faced him for the next day! Disgrace was everywhere. Should he leave it behind, where, at least, he would not hear and feel it? Should he, when all had turned from him, meet a brotherly welcome?

Then came back on him the thought of what Simon and Guy had made themselves; the thought of his father's grief at former doings of theirs, which had fallen so far short of the atrocity of this. He knew that his father had rather have seen each one of his five sons slain, or helpless cripples like the firstborn, than have been thus avenged. Nay, had he this morning prayed for the pardon of a crime, to which he would thus become a consenting party?

He looked up resolutely. "No, Hob Longbow. Hap what hap, my part can never be with those who have stained the Church with blood. Let my brothers know that my heart yearned to them before, but now all is over between us. I can only bear the doom they have brought upon me!"

It was not possible to remain and argue. A tent was a dangerous place for secret conferences, and Hob Longbow could only growl, "As you will, Sir. Now nor you nor any one else can say I have not done my charge."

"Alack, alack!" sighed Richard, "would that, my honour once redeemed, Hamlyn might make an end of me! But for thee, my poor Leonillo, I have no comforter or friend!" and he flung his arms round the dog's neck.

CHAPTER X—THE COMBAT

"And now with sae sharp of steele
They 'gan to lay on load."
Sir Cauline.

Heavy-hearted and pale-cheeked with his rigidly observed fast, Richard armed himself in early morning, and set forth to the chapel tent, where the previous solemnities had to be observed. He had made up his mind to make an earnest appeal to the Earl of Gloucester, for the sake of the old friendship with his father, to become his godfather in the combat, as one whose character stood too high to be injured by connection with him. Even this plan was frustrated, for Hamlyn de Valence entered, led by Earl Gilbert as his sponsor. Should he turn to his one other friend, the Prince himself? Nay, the Prince was umpire and judge. Never stood warrior so lonely. Little John of Dunster crept up to his side; and but for fear of injuring the child, he would almost have asked him to be his sponsor. At that moment, however, the tramp of horses' feet was heard, and Sir Reginald de Ferrieres, with his squires, galloped up to the tent.

The young Hospitalier held out his hand cordially. "In time, I hope," said he; "I have ridden ever since Lauds at Castel San Giovanni, hoping to be with you, so as to stand by you in this matter."

"It was kindly done of you," said Richard, tears of gratitude swelling in his eyes, as he wrung Sir Raynald's hand. "I have not even a godfather for the fight! How could you know of my need?"

"Some of our brethren came over from the camp, for our Ash Wednesday procession, and spoke of the stress you were in—that your Montfort lineage was out, and that you were thought to have writ a letter—but stay, there's no time for words; methinks here's the Prince and all his train."

Sir Raynald went through the solemnity of presenting Richard de Montfort as about to fight in defence of his own innocence. The Prince coldly accepted the presentation. Richard knew that Sir Raynald was deemed anything but a satisfactory sponsor; but the young knight's hearty sympathy, a sort of radiance caught from good old Sir Robert, was too comforting not to be reposed on.

Each champion then confessed. Raynald heard Richard's shrift, and nearly wept over it—it was the first the young priestly knight had received, and he could scarcely clear his voice to speak the words of absolution. Even as they left the confessional, he grasped Richard's hand and said, "Cast in thy lot with us! St. John will find thee father and home and brethren!"

And a gleam of joy and hope flashed on the youth's heart, and shone brighter as he participated in the solemn Mass in preparation for the combat. This over, each champion made oath of the justice of his quarrel in the hands of his godfather before the Prince: Hamlyn de Valence swearing that to the best of his belief, Richard de Montfort was a traitor, in league with his brothers, and art and part in the murder of Prince Henry of Almayne, and offering to prove it on his body; while on the other hand Richard swore that he was a true and faithful liegeman to the King, free from all intercourse with his brethren, and sackless of the death of Prince Henry.

Then each mounted on horseback, the trumpets sounded, the sponsors led them to their places, and the Prince's clear voice exclaimed, "And so God show the right." One glance of pitying sympathy would have filled Richard's arm with fresh vigour.

The two youths closed with shivered lances, and horses reeling from the shock. Backing their steeds, each received a fresh lance. Again they met; Richard felt the point of Hamlyn's lance glint against his breastplate, glide down, enter, make its way into his flesh; but at the same instant his lance was pushing, driving, bearing on Hamlyn before him; the sheer force in his Plantagenet shoulders was telling now, the very pain seemed as it were to add to the energy with which he pressed on—on, till the hostile spear dropped from his own side, and Hamlyn was borne backwards over the croup of the staggering horse, till he fell with crashing ringing armour upon the ground. Little John clapped his hands, and shouted for joy; but no one responded.

Richard leapt down in another second, and stood over him. "Yield thee, Hamlyn de Valence. Confess that thou hast slandered me with an ungrounded accusation."

Hamlyn had no choice. "Let me rise," he said sullenly; "I will confess, so thou letst me open my visor."

And Richard standing aside, Hamlyn spoke out in a dogged formal tone. "I hereby own, that by the judgment of Heaven, Richard de Montfort hath cleared himself of all share in the foul murder of Lord Henry, whose soul Heaven assoilzie. Also that he hath disproven the charge of leaguing with his brethren."

Richard was the victor, but where were the gratulations? Young John's hearty but slender hurrah was lost in the general silence.

The Prince reared his stately form, and said, "The judgment of Heaven is final. Richard de Montfort is pronounced free of all penalty for treason in the matter of the death of our dear cousin, and is free to go where he will."

Cold as ice was the Prince's face. That Richard meant murder to Henry, he had never believed; but that he had hankered after his brothers, and held dangerous communings with them, was evidently still credited and unforgiven. The very form of words was a dismissal—and the youth's heart was wrung.

He stood, looking earnestly up as the Prince moved from his place, without a glance towards him. The next moment Raynald's kind hand was on his shoulder, and his voice saying, "Well fought, brother, a brave stroke! Come with me, thou art hurt."

"Would it were to the death!" murmured Richard dreamily, as Raynald, throwing his arm round him, led him away; but before they had reached the tent there was a plunging rush and scampering behind them, and John of Dunster came dashing up. "I knew it! I knew it!" he cried. "I knew he would overset spiteful Hamlyn! Hurrah! They can't keep me away now, Richard— now the judgment of Heaven has gone for you!"

Richard smiled, and put his gauntleted hand caressingly on the boy's shoulder.

"I was afraid," added John, "that you would think me like the rest of them. Miscreants, all! Not one would shout for you—you, the victor! They don't heed the judgment of Heaven one jot. And that's what they call being warriors of the Cross! If the Prince were a true-born Englishman, he would be ashamed of himself. But never heed, Richard. Why don't you speak to me? Are you angered that I told of the letter? Indeed, I never guessed—"

"Hush, varlet," said Sir Raynald, "see you not that he has neither breath nor voice to speak? If you wish to do him a service, hie to our tents—down yonder, to the east, where you see the eight-pointed cross—"

"I know, Sir," said John, perfectly civil on hearing accents as English as his own.

"And bring up Brother Bartlemy, he is a better infirmarer than I. Bid him from me bring his salves and bandages."

Richard was barely conscious when he reached the tent, as much from rigid fasting and sleeplessness as from the actual loss of blood. His friend disarmed him tenderly, and revived him with bread and wine, silencing a half-murmured scruple about Lenten diet with the dispensation due to sickness. The wound was not likely to be serious or disabling, and the cares of the Hospitalier and his infirmarer had presently set their patient so much at ease that he dropped into a sound sleep, having scarcely said a word, beyond a few faintly uttered thanks, since he had fought the combat.

At first his sleep was profound, but by and by the associations of blows and wounds carried him back to the field of Evesham. The wild melee was renewed, he heard the voice of his father, but always in that strange distressing manner peculiar to dreams of the departed, always far away, and just beyond his reach, ever just about to give him the succour he needed, but ever withheld. The thunderstorm that broke over the contending armies roared again in his ears; and then again recurred the calm still night, when he had lain helpless on the battle-field; even the caress of Leonillo, and his low growl, were vividly repeated; but as the dog moved, it was to Richard as if the form of his father rose up in its armour from the dark field, and said in a deep hollow voice, "Well fought, my son; I will give thee knighthood." Then Richard thought he was kneeling before his father, and hearing that same voice saying, "My son, be true and loyal. In the name of God and St. James. I dub thee knight of death!" and looking up, he beheld under the helmet, not Simon de Montfort's face but the Prince's. He awoke with a start of disappointment—and there stood Edward himself, leaning against the tent-pole, looking down at him!

He sprang on his feet, scarcely knowing whether he slept or woke; but Edward said, in that voice that at times was so ineffably sweet, "Be still, Richard; I fear me thou hast suffered a wrong, and I am come to repair it, as far as I can! Lay thee down again."

And the Prince seated himself on the oaken chest; while Richard, after a few words, sat down on his couch.

"Is this the letter about which there has been such a coil?" said Edward, giving him the scroll in its sepia ink.

"It is!" replied Richard in amazement and dismay.

"The only letter thou didst write?"

"The only one," repeated Richard.

"And," added Edward, "it concerns thy brother Henry."

Richard turned even paler than before, and could not suppress a gasp of dismay. "My Lord, make me not forsworn!"

"Listen to me, Richard," said Edward. "My sweet lady gave me no rest about thee. She held that I had withdrawn my trust over lightly, for what was no blame to thine heart; and that having set thee here apart from thy natural friends, we owed thee more notice than I have been wont to think wholesome for untried striplings. Others, and I among them, held that Raynald Ferrers' friendship and countenance showed thee stubbornly set on old connections, and many thought the letter to the Grand Prior Darcy a mere excuse. But when Hamlyn fell, and I still held that thou wert merely cleared from wilful share in the deadly crime of which I had never held thee guilty, then she spake more earnestly. She of her own will sent for Raynald Ferrers to our tent, and called me to speak with him, sure that, even though his family had been our foes, he was too honourable a knight to have espoused thy cause without good reason. Then it was that he told us of thine interest for the blind beggar whose child thou didst save, and of the Grand Prior's message. Also, as full exculpation of thee, he gave me the letter, which, having failed to find a home-bound messenger at San Giovanni, he had brought back to the camp. And now, Richard, what can I say more, than that I did thee wrong, and pray thee to give me thy hand in pardon?"

Richard hid his face and sobbed, completely overwhelmed by the simple dignity of the humility of such a man as Edward. He held the Prince's hand to his lips, and exclaimed, "Oh, how—how could I have ever felt discontent, or faltered? not in truth—oh, no—but in trust and patience? Oh! my Lord, that I could die for you!"

"Not yet," said Edward, smiling; "we have much to do together first. And now tell me, Richard, this beggar is indeed Henry?"

Richard hung his head.

"What, thou mayst not betray him?"

"I am under an oath, my Lord."

"Nay, I know well-nigh all, Richard. I did indeed see my dear old comrade laid in Evesham Church, so as it broke my heart to see him, bleeding from many wounds, and even his hand lopped by the savage Mortimers. Then, as I bent down, and gave his brow a last kiss, it struck me, for a moment, that the touch was not that of a dead man's skin. But I looked again at the deadly wounds of head and breast, and thought it would be but cruelty to strive to bring back the glimmer of life only to—to see the ruin of his house; and all that he could not be saved from. O Richard, to no man in either host could the day of Evesham have been so sore, as to me, who had to sit in the gate, to gladden men's hearts, like holy King David, when he would fain have been weeping for his son! But in early morning came Abbot William of Whitchurch to my chamber, and with much secrecy told me that the corpse of Henry de Montfort had been stolen from the church by night, praying me to excuse that the monks, wearied out with the day of alarms, and the care of our wounded, had not kept better watch. Then knew I that some one had been less faithless than I, and I hoped that poor Henry was at least dying in peace; I had never deemed that he could survive. But when I saw thy billet, and heard Ferrers' tale, I had no further doubt, remembering likewise how strangely familiar was the face of that little one at Westminster."

"Yes, my Lord, it was even as a strange, wild, wilful, blind beggar that I found poor Henry; and heavy was the curse he laid me under, should I make him known to you. He calls himself thus a freer and happier man than he could be even were he pardoned and reinstated; and he can indulge his vein of mockery."

"I dare be sworn that consoles him for all," said Edward, nearly laughing. "So long as he could utter his gibe, Henry little recked which way the world passed round him; and I trow he has found some mate of low degree, that he would be loth to produce in open day."

"Not so, my Lord: it is so wild a tale of true love that I can sometimes scarce believe a minstrel did not sing it to me!" And Richard told the history of Isabel Mortimer's fidelity. The Prince was deeply touched, and then remembered the marked manner in which the Baron of Mortimer had replied to his inquiry, in what convent he had bestowed Henry de Montfort's betrothed. "She is dead, my Lord, dead to us." Then he added suddenly, "So that black-eyed babe is the heiress of Leicester and all the honours of Montfort!"

"It is one of the causes for Henry's resolve to be secret," said Richard. "I thought it harsh and distrustful then, but he dreaded Simon's knowledge of her."

"We will find a way of securing her from Simon," said the Prince. "But fear not, Richard, Henry's secret shall be safe with me! I have kept his secrets before now," he added, with a smile. "Only, when we are at home again—so it please the Saints to spare us—thou shalt strive to show him cause to trust my Lady with his child, if he doth not seek to breed her up to scrip and wallet. I see such is thy counsel in this scroll, and it is well."

"How could I say other?" said Richard, "and now, more than ever! I long to thank the gracious Princess this very evening."

"Thy wound?' said the Prince.

"My wound is naught, I scarce feel it."

"Then," said the Prince, "unless the leech gainsay it, it would be as well to be at our pavilion this evening, that men may see thou art not in any disgrace. Rest then till supper-time." And as he spoke he rose to depart, but Richard made a gesture of entreaty. "So please your Grace, grant me a few farther words. I sware, and truly, that I had heard nothing from my brothers when I was accused of writing that letter to them. But see here, what yester-morn was pinned to that tent-pole."

He gave Edward the scroll, at which the Prince looked half smiling. "So! A dagger in store for me too, is there? Well, my cousins have a goodly thirst for vengeance! Hast thou any suspicion how this billet came here?"

"Ay, my Lord; and for that cause I would warn you against two of the archers, one of whom was in Simon's troop, and went with the late prince to Viterbo. I gave them no promise of silence."

"You spoke with them?"

"With one, who was charged to let me through the outposts to a spot where means were provided for bringing me to Guy."

"And thou," said Edward, smiling, "didst choose to bide the buffet?"

"Sir," said Richard, "I did indeed long after my brethren when Guy had been so near me in Africa; but now, I would far rather die than cast in my lot with them."

"Thou art wise," said Edward; "not merely right, but wise. I have sent Gloucester to my uncle of Sicily with such messages that he will scarce dare to leave them scatheless! Then, at supper-time we meet again—in thine own name, Richard, and as my kinsman and esquire. Thou shalt bear thine own name and arms. I will cause a mourning suit to be sent to thee—thou art equally of kin with myself to poor Henry—and shalt mourn him with Edmund and me at the requiem to- morrow. So will it best be manifest to the camp, that we exempt thee from all blame." Again he was departing, when Richard added—"The archers, my Lord—were it not good to dismiss them?"

"Tush," said Edward; "tell me not their names. So soon as the wind veers, they will be beyond Guy's reach; and if I were to stand on my guard against every man who loved thy father better than mine, what good would my life do me? The poor knaves will be true enough when they see a Saracen before them!"

And away went Edward, to be glanced at as he passed through the camp, as a severe, hard, cruel tyrant. Had he only been gay, open-hearted, and careless, he might have hung both the guilty archers, and a dozen innocent ones into the bargain, and yet have never won the character for harshness and unmercifulness that he had acquired even while condoning many a dire offence, simply from his stern gravity, and his punctilious exactitude in matters of discipline. But the evils of a lax and easy-going court had been so fatal, and had produced such suffering, that it was no marvel that he had adopted a rule of iron; and in the pain and distress of seeing his closest friends, the noblest subjects in the realm, pushed into a rebellion where he had himself to maintain his father's cause, and then to watch, without being able to hinder, the mean-spirited revenge of his own partizans, his manner had acquired that silent reserve and coldness which made him feared and hated by the many, while intensely beloved by the few. Even towards those few it was absolutely difficult to him to unbend, as he had done in this hour of effusion towards Richard; and the youth was proportionably moved and agitated with fervent gratitude and affection.

He had scarcely had so happy an evening since he had been a boy at Odiham. He was indeed feeble and dizzy at times, but with a far from painful languor; and the Princess, enjoying the permission to follow the dictates of her own heart, was kind to him with a motherly or sisterly kindness, could not bear to receive from him his wonted attendance, but made him lie upon the cushions at her feet, and when out of hearing of every one, talked of the faithful Isabel, and of "pretty Bessee," on whom she already looked as the companion of her little Eleanor, whom she had left at home.

It might be questioned whether Richard did not undergo more in watching little John de Mohun's endeavours at waiting than he would have suffered from doing it himself. And not a few dissatisfied glances were levelled at the favoured stripling, besides the literally as well as figuratively sour glances of Dame Idonea.

Edward, being of course unable to betray his real grounds for acquitting Richard, had only deigned to inform Prince Edmund that he knew all, and was perfectly satisfied. Now Prince Edmund, as well as all the old court faction, deemed Edward's regard for the Barons' party an unreasonable weakness that they durst not indeed combat openly, but which angered them as a species of disaffection to his own cause. The outer world thought him a tyrant, but there was an inner world to whom he appeared weakly good-natured and generous; and this inner world thought Richard had successfully hoodwinked him!

Therefore Edmund of Lancaster desired to adopt Hamlyn de Valence as his own squire, to save him from association with Richard; and both prince and squire, and all the rest of the train, made it perfectly evident to the young Montfort that he was barely tolerated out of respect for the Prince.

But Richard in his joy could have borne worse than this, for the Prince had not relaxed in his kindness, and made his young cousin's wound an excuse for showing him more tenderness and consideration than he would otherwise have thought befitting. Moreover, an esquire, as Richard had now become, might be in much closer relations of intimacy with his master than was possible to a page; and the day that had begun so sadly was like the dawn of a brighter period.

Sir Raynald Ferrers had been invited to the Prince's pavilion, but the rules of his Order did not permit his joining a secular entertainment in Lent, and he did not admit either the camp life or the gravity of the Prince's mourning household as a dispensation. However, when Richard, leaning fondly on little John's ready shoulder, crossed to his own tent, he found his good friend waiting there to attend to his wound, which Sir Raynald professed to regard as an excellent subject to practise upon, and likewise to hear whether all had been cleared up, and had gone right with him.

"Though," he said, "I could not doubt of it when that fair and lovely Princess had taken your matters in hand. Tell me, Richard, have you secular men many such dames as that abroad in the world?"

"Not many such as she," said Richard, smiling.

"Well, I have not spoken to a female thing, save perhaps pretty Bessee, since I went into the Spital, ten years ago; and verily the sound of the lady's voice was to me as if St. Margaret had begun talking to me! And so wise and clear of wit too. I thought women were feather-pated wilful beings, from whom there was no choice but to shut oneself up! I trow, that now all is well with thee, thou wilt scarce turn a thought again towards our brotherhood, where to glance at such a being becomes a sin." And Raynald crossed himself, with an effort to recall his wonted asceticism.

"Ladies' love is not like to be mine," said Richard, laughing, as one not yet awake to the force of the motive. "No! Gladly would I be one of your noble brotherhood, where alone have I met with kindness— but, Sir Raynald, my first duty under Heaven must be to redeem my father's name, by my service to the Prince. My brothers think they uphold it by deadly revenge. I want to show what a true Montfort can be with such a master as my father never had! And, Raynald, I cannot but fear that further schemes of vengeance may be afloat. The Prince is too fearless to take heed to himself, and who is so bound to watch for him as I?"

CHAPTER XI—THE VIEW FROM CARMEL

"On her who knew that love can conquer death;
  Who, kneeling with one arm about her king,
Drew forth the poison with her balmy breath,
    Sweet as new buds in spring."—TENNYSON.

A year had elapsed since the crusaders had landed in Palestine; Nazareth had been taken, and the Christian host were encamped upon the plain before Acre, according to their Prince's constant habit of preferring to keep his troops in the open field, rather than to expose them to the temptations of the city— which was, alas! in a state most unworthy of the last stronghold of Latin Christianity in the Holy Land.

It was on a scorching June day, Whitsun Tuesday, in the exquisite beauty of an early summer in the mountains of the Levant—when "the flowers appear on the earth, the time of the singing of birds is come, and the voice of the turtle is heard in our land; the fig tree putteth forth her green figs, and the vines with the tender grape give a good smell,"—that Richard de Montfort was descending the wooded sides of Mount Carmel.

Anxious tidings had of late come from England respecting the health of the little Prince John; and Princess Eleanor was desirous of offering gifts and obtaining prayers on his behalf, on the part of the good Fathers of the convent associated with the memory of the great Prophet who had raised the dead child to life. She herself, however, was at the time unfit for a mountain ride; and Prince Edward, who was a lay brother of the Carmelite order, and had fully intended himself to go and offer his devotions for his child, was so unwell on that day, from the feverish heat of the summer, that he could not expose himself to the sun; and Richard was therefore despatched on the part of the royal pair. He had ascended in the cool of the morning, setting forth before sunrise, and attending the regular Mass. The good Fathers would fain have detained him till the heat of the day should be past; but his anxiety not to overpass in the slightest degree the time fixed by the Prince, made him resolved on setting out so soon as his errand was sped.

Unspeakably beautiful was his ride—through rocky dells filled with copsewood, among which jessamine, lilies, and exquisite flowers were peeping up, and the coney, the fawn, and other animals, made Leonillo prick his ears and wistfully seek from his master's eye permission to dash off in pursuit. Or the "oaks of Carmel," with many a dark- leaved evergreen, towered in impenetrable thicket, and at an opening glade might be beheld on the north-east, "that goodly mountain Lebanon" rising in a thick clothing of wood; and beyond, in sharp cool softness, the white cone of rain-distilling Hermon. Far to the west lay the glorious glittering sheet of the Mediterranean; but nearer, almost beneath his feet, was the curving bay and harbour of Ptolemais, filled with white sails, the white city of Acre full of fortresses and towers; while on the plain beside it, green with verdure as Richard's own home greenwood of Odiham, lay the white tents of the Christian army, in so clear an atmosphere that he could see the flash of the weapons of the men on guard, and almost distinguish the blazonry of the banners.

Richard dismounted to gather some roses and jessamine for the Princess, and to collect some of the curious fossil echini, which he believed to be olives turned to stone by the Prophet Elijah, as a punishment to a churlish peasant who refused him a meal. He thought that such treasures would be a welcome addition to the store he was accumulating for the good old Grand Prior. He gave his horse to Hob Longbow, his only attendant except a young Sicilian lad. This same Longbow had stuck to him with a pertinacity that he could not shake off, and in truth had hitherto justified the Prince's prediction that he would be a brave and faithful fellow when his allegiance was no further disturbed by the proximity of the outlawed Montforts. There had been nothing to lead Richard to think he ought to indicate either him or Nick Dustifoot to the Prince as the persons who had been connected with Guy in Italy.

Presently Leonillo bounded forward, and Richard became aware of the figure of a man in light armour standing partly hidden among the brushwood, but looking down intently into the Christian camp. The dog leapt up, fawning on the stranger with demonstrations of rapture; and he, turning in haste, stood face to face with Richard.

"Here!" was his exclamation, and a grasp was instantly laid upon his sword.

"Simon!" burst from Richard's lips at the same moment, "dost not know me?"

"Thou, boy?" and the hold was relaxed. "What lucky familiar sent thee hither? What—thou art grown such a huge fellow that I had well-nigh struck thee down for Longshanks himself, had it not been for thy voice. Thou hast his very bearing."

"Simon!" again repeated Richard, in his extremity of amazement. "What dost thou? How camest thou here? Whence—?"

"That thou shalt soon see," said Simon. "A right free and merry home and company have we up yonder,"—and he pointed towards Mount Lebanon.

"Thou and Guy?"

"No, no; Guy turned craven. Could not endure our wanderings in the marshes and hills, pined for his wife forsooth, fell sick, and must needs go and give himself up to the Pope; so he sings the penitential psalms night and day."

"And we heard thou wast dead at Siena."

"Thou hearest many a false tale," said Simon. "Of my death thou shalt judge, if thou wilt turn thy horse and ride with me to our hill-fort of Ain Gebel, in Galilee. They say 'tis the very one which King David or King Herod, whichever it was, could only take by letting down his men-at-arms in boxes! I should like to see the boxes that we could not send skimming down the abyss! And a wondrous place they have left us—vaults as cool as a convent wine-cellar, fountains out of the rock, marble columns."

"But, brother, for whom do you hold it? For the King of Cyprus or— ?"

"For myself, boy! For King Simon, an it like you better! None can touch me or my merry band there, and a goodly company we are— pilgrims grown wiser, and runaway captives, and Druses, and bold Arabs too: and the choicest of many a heretic Armenian merchants' caravan is ours, and of many a Saracen village; corn and wine, fair dames, and Damascus blades, and Arab steeds. Nothing has been wanting to me but thee and vengeance, and both are, I hope, on the way!"

"Not I, certainly!" said Richard, shrinking back in horror: "I—a sworn crusader!"

"Tush, what are we but crusaders too, boy? 'Tis all service against the Moslem! Thy patron saint sent thee to me to-day from special care for thy safety."

"How so!" exclaimed Richard. "If peril threaten my Lord, I must be with him at once."

"Much hast thou gained by hanging on upon him," said Simon scornfully, glancing at Richard's heels; "not so much as a pair of gilt spurs! Creeping after him like a hound, thou hast not even the bones!"

"I have all I seek," said Richard. "I have his brotherly kindness. I have the opportunity of redeeming my name. Nay, I should even regret any honour that took me from the services I now perform.

Simon, didst thou but know his love for our father!"

"Silence, base caitiff!" thundered Simon; "I know his deeds, and that is enough for me! Look here, mean-spirited as thou wert to be taken with his hypocrisy, I have pity on thee yet. I would spare thee what awaits thee in the camp!"

"For heaven's sake, Simon, dost know of any attack of the Emir? The Princess must at once be conveyed into the town! As thou art a man, a Christian, speak plainly!"

"Foolish lad, the infidels are quiet enough! No peril threatens the camp! Only if thou wilt run thy head into it, thou art like to find it too hot to hold thee!"

"I am afraid of no accusations," said Richard; "my Lord knows and trusts me."

Simon laughed a loud ringing scornful laugh.

"Wilful will to water," he said. "Well, thou besotted lad, if it be not too late when thou getst into the hands of Crookbacked Edmund and Red Gilbert, remember the way to Galilee, that is all!"

"I tell thee, Simon," said Richard, turning round and fully facing him; "I would rather perish an innocent man by the hands of the Provost Marshal, than darken my soul with thy counsels of blood. O Simon! What thy purpose may be I know not; but canst thou deem it faithfulness to our father, saint as he was, to live this dark wild life, so utterly abhorrent to him?"

"Let those look to that who slew him, and made me such as I am," returned Simon, turning from him, and gazing steadfastly down into the camp. Suddenly a gleam of fierce exultation lighted up his face, and again facing Richard he exclaimed, "Yes, go home, tame cringing spaniel, and see whether a Montfort is still in favour below there! See if proud Edward is still ready to meet thy fawning with his scornful patronage! See if the honour of a murdered father has not been left in better hands than thine! And when thou hast had thy lesson, find the way to Ain Gebel, or ask Nick Dustifoot."

Richard, with a startled exclamation, looked down, but could discern nothing unusual in the camp. The royal banner hung in heavy folds over the Prince's pavilions, and all was evidently still in the same noontide repose, or rather exhaustion, to which the Syrian sun reduced even the hardy active Englishmen. "What mean you?" he began; but Simon was no longer beside him. He called, but echo alone answered; and all he could do was to throw himself on his horse, and hurry down the mountain side, with a vague presentiment of evil, and a burning desire to warn his lord or share his peril.

He understood Simon's position. Many of the almost inaccessible rocks, where the sons of Anak had built their Cyclopean fortresses, and which had been abodes of almost fabulous beauty and strength in the Herodian days, had been resorted to again by the crusaders, and had served as isolated strongholds whence to annoy the enemy. Frightfully lawless had, in too many instances, been the life there led, more especially by the Levant-born sons of Europeans; and in the universal disorganization of the Kingdom of Jerusalem, that took place in consequence of the disputed rights of Cyprus and Hohenstaufen, most of them had become free from all control. If the garrisons bore the Christian name at all, it chiefly was as an excuse for preying on all around; but too often they were renegades of every variety of nation, drawn together by the vilest passions, commanded by some reckless adventurer, and paying a species of allegiance to any power that either endangered them, or afforded them the hopes of plunder. Bloodthirsty and voluptuous alike, they were viewed with equal terror by the Frank pilgrim, the Syriac villager, the Armenian merchant, and the Saracen hadji—whose ransom and whose spoil enriched their chambers, with all that the licentious tastes of East and West united could desire. There were comparatively few of these nests of iniquity in these latter days of the Crusades, but some still survived; and Richard had seen some of their captains with their followers at the siege of Nazareth, where the atrocities they had committed had been such as to make the English army stand aghast. As a member of such a crew, Simon could hardly fail to find means of attempting that revenge on which it was but too evident that he was still bent; and Richard, as every possible risk rose before him, urged his horse to perilous speed down the steep descent, and chid every obstacle, though in fact the descent which ordinarily occupied two hours, for men who cared for their own necks, was effected by him in a quarter of the time. He came to the entrenched camp. The entrance, where the Prince made so strict a point of keeping a sentinel, was completely unguarded. The foremost tents were empty, but there was a sound as of the murmuring voices of numbers towards the centre of the camp. The next moment he met Hamlyn de Valence riding quickly, and followed by two attendants.

"Hamlyn! a moment!" he gasped. "Has aught befallen the Prince?"

"You were aware of it, then!" said Hamlyn, checking his horse, and looking him full in the face.

"Answer me, for Heaven's sake! Is all well with the Princes?"

"As well as your house desires—or it may be somewhat better," said Hamlyn; "but let me pass. I am on an errand of life or death."

So saying, Hamlyn dashed forwards; and Richard, in double alarm, made his way to the space in the centre of the camp, where he found himself on the outskirts of a crowd, talking in the various tongues of English, French, and Lingua Franca. "He lives—the good Princess- -the dogs of infidels—poison —" were the words he caught. He flung himself from his horse, and was about to interrogate the nearest man, when John of Dunster came hurrying towards him from the tents, and threw himself upon him, sobbing with agitation and dismay.

"What is it? Speak, John! The Prince!"

"Oh, if you had but been there! It will not cease bleeding. O Richard, he looks worse than my father when he came home!"

"Let me hear! Where? How is he hurt?"

"In the arm and brow," said the boy.

"The arm!" said Richard, much relieved.

"Ah, but they say the dagger is poisoned! Stay, Richard, I'll tell you all. Dame Idonea turned me out of the tent, and she will not let any one in. It was thus— even now the Prince was lying on the day- bed in his own outer tent, no one else there save myself. I believe everybody was asleep, I know I was—when Nick Dustifoot called me, and bade me tell the Prince there was a messenger from the Emir of Joppa, asking to see him. So the Prince roused himself up, and bade him come in. He was one of those quick-eyed Moorish-looking infidels, in the big turbans and great goat's hair cloaks; and he went down on his knees, and hit the ground with his forehead, and said Salam aleikum— traitor that he was—and gave the Prince a letter. Well, the Prince muttered something about his head aching so sorely that he could scarce see the writing, and had just put up his hand to shade his eyes from the light, when the dog was out with a dagger and fell on him! The Prince's arm being raised, caught the stroke, you see; and that moment his foot was up," said John, acting the kick, "and down went the rogue upon his back! And I—I threw myself right down over him!"

"Did you, my brave little fellow? Well done of you!" cried Richard.

"And the Prince wrested the dagger out of the rogue's hand, only he tore his own forehead sorely, as the point flew up with the shock— and then stabbed the villain to the heart—see how the blood rushed over me! Then the Prince pulled me up, and called me a brave lad, and set me on my feet, and asked me if I were sure I was not hurt. And by that time the archers were coming in, when all was over; and Long Robin must needs snatch up a joint stool and have a stroke at the Moor's head. I trow the Prince was wrath with the cowardly clown for striking a dead man. He said I alone had been any aid!"

"'Well?" anxiously asked Richard, gathering intense alarm as he saw that the boy's trouble still exceeded his elation, even at such commendation as this.

"But then," said John sadly, "even while he called it nothing, there came a dizziness over him. And even then the Princess had heard the outcry, and came in haste with Dame Idonea. And so soon as the Dame had picked up the dagger and looked well at it, and smelt it, she said there was poison on it. No sooner did the Princess hear that, than, without one word, she put her lips to his arm to suck forth the venom. He was for withholding her, but the Dame said that was the only safeguard for his life; and she looked—oh, so imploring!"

"Blessings on the sweet Princess and true wife!" cried the men-at-arms, great numbers of whom had gathered round the little eye-witness to hear his account.

"And so is he saved?" said Richard, with a long breath.

"Ah! but," said John, his eyes beginning to fill with tears, "there is the Grand Master of the Templars come now, and he says that to suck the poison is of no avail; and that nothing will save him but cutting away the living flesh as I would carve the wing of a bustard; and Dame Idonea says that is just the way King Coeur de Lion died, and the Princess is weeping, and the wound will not stop bleeding; and Hamlyn is gone to Acre for a surgeon, and they are all wrangling, and Dame Idonea boxed my ears at last, and said I was gaping there." The boy absolutely burst into sobs and tears, and at the same moment a growl arose among the archers, of "Curses on the Moslem hounds! Not one shall escape! Death to every captive in our hands!"

"Nay, nay," exclaimed Richard, looking up in horror; "the poor captives are utterly guiltless! Far more justly make me suffer," murmured he sadly.

"All tarred with the same stick," said the nearest; "serve them as they deserve."

"Think," added Richard, "if the Prince would see no dishonour done to the dead carcase of the murderer himself, would he be willing to have ill worked on living men, sackless of the wrong? English turning butchers—that were fit work for Paynims."

"No, no, not one shall live to laugh at our Edward's fall," burst out the men; and a voice among them added, "Sure the young squire seems to know a vast deal about the guilty and the guiltless—the Montfort! Ay! Away with all foes to our Edward—"

"Best withdraw yourself, Sir," said Hob Longbow; "their blood is up. Baulk them of their prey, and they will set on you next."

Richard just then beheld a person from whose interposition he had much greater hopes, namely the Earl of Gloucester, who, though still a young man, was the chief English noble in the camp, and whose special charge the Saracen captives were. He hurried towards him, and asked tidings of the Prince.

"Ill tidings, I trow," said the Earl, bitterly. "Ay, Richard de Montfort, you had best take heed to yourself, he was your best friend; and a sore lookout it is for us all. Between the old dotard his father and the poor babes his children, England is in woeful plight. Would that your father's wits were among us still! There's some curse on this fools' errand of a Crusade, for here is the sixth prince it hath slain, and well if we lose not our Princess too. But what is all this uproar!"

"The men-at-arms, my Lord," said Richard, "fierce to visit the crime on the captives."

"A good riddance!" said Earl Gilbert; "the miscreants eat as much as ten score yeomen, and my knaves are weary with guarding them. If this matter brings all the pagans in Palestine on our hands, we shall have enough to do without looking after this nest of heathens."

"But would the Prince have it so?"

"I fear me the Prince is like to have little will in the matter! No, no, I'm not the man to order a butchery, but if the honest fellows must needs shed blood for blood, I'm not going to meddle between them and the heathen wolves."

Assuredly nothing was to be done with the Red de Clare, and Richard pushed on, with throbbing dismayed heart, to the tent, dreading to behold the condition of him whom he best loved and honoured on earth. The tent was crowded, but Richard's unusual height enabled him to see, over the heads of those nearest, that Edward was sitting on the edge of his couch, his wife and Dame Idonea endeavouring to check the flow of blood from his wound. The elbow of his other arm was on his knee, and his head on his hand, but the opening of the curtain let in the light; he looked up, and Richard saw how deathly white his face had become, and the streaks of blood from the scratch upon his brow. He greeted Richard, however, with the look of recognition to which his young squire had now become used—not exactly a smile, but a well-satisfied welcome; and though he spoke low and feebly to his brother who stood near him, Richard caught the words with a thrill of emotion.

"Let him near me, Edmund. He hath a ready hand, and may aid thee, sweet wife. Thou art wearying thyself." Then, as Richard approached, "Thou hast sped well! I looked not for thee so soon."

"Alack, my Lord!" said Richard, "I hurried on to warn you. Ah! would I had been in time!"

"Thy little pupil, John, did all man could do," said Edward, languidly smiling. "But what—hast aught in charge to say to me? Be brief, for I am strangely dizzy."

"My Lord," said Richard, "the archers and men-at-arms are furiously wrath with the Saracens. They would wreak their vengeance on the prisoners, who at least are guiltless!"

"The knaves!" exclaimed Edward promptly. "Why looks not Gloucester to this?"

"My Lord, the Earl saith that he would not command the slaughter, but that he will not forbid it."

"Saints and angels!" burst forth the Prince, and to the amazement of all, he started at once on his feet, and striding through the bystanders to the opening of the tent, he looked out on the crowd, who were already rushing towards the inclosure where their victims were penned. Raising his mighty voice as in a battle-day, he called aloud to them to halt, turn back, and hear him. They turned, and beheld the lofty form in the entrance of the tent, wrapped in a long loose robe, which, as well as his hair, was profusely stained with blood, his wan face, however, making that marble dignity and sternness of his even more awful and majestic as he spoke aloud. "So, men, you would have me go down to my grave blood-stained and accursed by the death of guiltless captives? And I pray you, what is to be the lot of our countrymen, now on pilgrimage to Jerusalem, if you thus deal with our prisoners, taken in war? Senseless bloody- minded hounds that ye are, mark my words. The life of one of you for the life of a Saracen captive; and should I die, I lay my curse on ye all, if every man of them be not set free the hour my last breath is drawn. Do you hear me, ye cravens?"

Unsparing, unconciliatory as ever, even when most merciful and generous, Edward turned, but reeled as he re-entered the tent, and his dizziness recurring, needed the support of both his brother and Richard to lay him down on the couch.

The Grand Master of the Temple renewed his assurance that this was a token of the poison, and Eleanor was unheeded when she declared that her dear lord had been affected in the same manner before his wound, ever since indeed the Whit Sunday when he had ridden home from the great Church of St. John of Acre in the full heat of the sun.

Dame Idonea was muttering the mediaeval equivalent for fiddlesticks, as plain as her respect for the Temple would allow her.

At that moment the leech whom Hamlyn had been sent into the town to summon, made his appearance, and fully confirmed the Templar's opinion. Neither the wizened Greek physician, nor the dignified Templar, considered the soft but piteous assurance of the wife that the venom had at once been removed by her own lips as more than mere feminine folly, and Dame Idonea's real experience of knights thus saved, and on the other hand of the fatal consequences of rude surgery in such a climate, were disregarded as an old woman's babble. Her voice waxed shrill and angry, and her antagonists' replies in Lingua Franca, mixed with Arabic, Latin, and Greek, rang through the tent, till the Prince could bear it no longer.

"Peace," he said, with an asperity unlike his usual stern patience, "I had liefer brook your knives than your tongues! Without further jangling, tell me clearly, learned physician, the peril of either submitting or not submitting to your steel."

The Greek told, with as little tergiversation as was in his nature, that he viewed a refusal as certain death, but several times Dame Idonea was bursting out upon him, and Edward had to hold up his finger to silence her.

"Now, kind lady," quoth he, "let me hear the worst you foretell for me from your experience."

Dame Idonea did not spare him either the fate of Coeur de Lion, the dangers of fever and pain, and above all "of that strange enchantment that binds the teeth together and forbids a man to swallow his food." Poor Eleanor looked at him imploringly all the time, but as none of them had ever heard of the circulation of the blood, they could not tell that her simple remedy had been truly efficacious, and that if it had been otherwise the incisions would now come too late. Thus the balance of prudence made itself appear to be on the side of the physician, and for him the Prince decided. "Mi Dona," he said, ever his most caressing term for her, "it must be so! I think not lightly of what thou hast done for me, but, as matters stand, too much hangs upon this life of mine for me not to be bound to run no needless risk for fear of a little pain. If I live and speak now, next to highest Heaven it is owing to thee; and when we came on this holy war, sweet Eleanor, didst thou not promise to hinder me from naught that a true warrior of the Cross ought to undergo? And is this the land to shrink from the Cross?"

Alas! to Eleanor the pang was the belief in the uselessness of his suffering and danger. She never withstood his will, but physically she was weak, and her weeping was piteous in its silence. Edward bade his brother lead her away; and Edmund, after the usual fashion, vented his own perplexity and distress upon the most submissive person in his way. He assumed more resistance on the part of his gentle sister-in-law than she made, and carrying her from the tent, roughly told her, silent as she was, that it was better that she should scream and cry than all England wail and lament.

And so Eleanor's devoted deed, the true saving of her husband, has lived on as a mere delusive tradition, weakly credited by the romantic, while the credit of his recovery has been retained by the Knight-Templars' leech. Not a sound was uttered by the Prince while under those hands; but when his wife was permitted to return to him, she found him in a dead faint, and the silver reliquary she had left with him crushed flat and limp between his fingers.

Richard had given his attendance all the time, and for several hours afterwards, during which the Princess hung over her husband, endeavouring to restore him from the state of exhaustion in which he scarcely seemed conscious of anything but her presence. Late in the evening, some one came to the entrance of the tent, and beckoned to the young squire; he came out expecting to receive some message, but to his extreme surprise found himself in the grasp of the Provost Marshal.

"On what charge?" he demanded, so soon as he was far enough beyond the precincts of his tent not to risk a disturbance.

"By the command of the council. On the charge of being privy to the attempt on the Prince's life."

"By whom preferred?" asked Richard.

"By the Lord Hamlyn de Valence."

Richard attempted not another word. In effect the condition of the Prince seemed to him so hopeless that his most acute suffering at the moment was in the being prevented from ministering to him, or watching for a last word or look of recognition. He had no heart for self-vindication, even if he had not known its utter futility with men who had been prejudiced against him from the outset. Nor had he the opportunity, for the Provost Marshal conducted him at once to the tent where he was to be in ward for the night, a heap of straw for him to lie upon, and a guard of half a dozen archers outside; and there was he left to his despairing prayers for the Prince's life. He could dwell on nothing else, there was no room in his mind for any thought but of that glory of manhood thus laid low, and of the anguish of the sweet face of the Princess.

"Sir—!" there was a low murmur near him—"now is the time. I have brought an archer's gown and barrett, and we may easily get past the yeomen." These last words were uttered, as on hands and knees a figure whose dark outline could barely be discerned, crept under the border of the tent.

"Who art thou?" hastily inquired Richard.

"You should know me, Sir,—I have done you many a good turn, and served your house truly."

"Talk not of truth, thou traitor," said Richard, recognizing Dustifoot's voice. "Knowst thou that but for the Prince's clemency thou hadst a year ago been out of the reach of the cruel evil thou hast now shared in."

"Nay, now, Lord Richard," returned the man, "you should not treat thus an honest fellow that would fain do you service."

"I need no service such as thine," returned Richard. "Thy service has made my brothers murderers, and brought ruin and woe unspeakable upon the land."

"Beshrew me," muttered the man, "but one would have thought the young damoiseau would have had more feeling about his father's death! But I swore to do Sir Simon's bidding, so that is no concern of mine; and he bade me, if any one strove to lay hands on you, Sir, to lead you down to Kishon Brook, where he will meet us with a plump of spears."

"Meet him then," said Richard, "and say to him that if from his crag above, on Carmel, he sees me hung on the gallows tree as a traitor, he may count that I am willingly offered for our family sin! Ay, and that if he thinks an old man's hairs brought down to the grave, a broken-hearted wife, helpless orphans, and a land without a head, to be a grateful offering to my father, let him enjoy the thought of how the righteous Earl would have viewed all the desolation that will fall on England without the one—one scholar who knew how to value and honour his lessons."

"Hush! Sir," hastily interposed Dustifoot; but it was too late, the murmur of voices had already been caught by the guard, and quick as he was to retreat, their torches discovered him as he was creeping out, and he was dragged back by the feet, and the light held up to his face, while many voices proclaimed him as the rogue who had been foremost in admitting the assassin to the royal tent. It was from the tumult of voices that Richard first understood that on examining the body of the murderer, it had been ascertained that he was neither a Bedouin nor one of the assassins belonging to the Old Man of the Mountain, but an European, probably a Provencal; and this, added to Hamlyn's representation of Richard's words, together with what the Earls of Lancaster and Gloucester recollected, had directed the suspicion upon himself. And here was, as it seemed, undeniable evidence of his connection with the plot!

The miserable Dustifoot, vainly imploring his intercession, was tied hand and foot, and the guard returned to the outside of the tent, except one archer, who thought it needful to bring in his torch, and keep the prisoners in sight.

The night passed wearily, and with morning Dustifoot was removed to a place of captivity more befitting his degree; but of the Prince, Richard only heard that he continued to be in great danger. No attempt on the part of the council was made to examine their prisoner; and Richard suspected, as time wore on, that no one chose to act in this time of suspense for fear of incurring the lion-like wrath of Edward in the event of his recovery, but that in case of his death, small would be his own chances of life. Death had fewer horrors for the lonely boy than it would have had for one with whom life had been brighter. In battle for the Cross, or in shielding his Prince's life, it would have been welcome, but death, branded with vile ingratitude, as a traitor to that master, was abhorrent. Shrunk up in the corner of the tent, half asleep after the night's vigil, yet too miserable for the entire oblivion of rest, Richard spent the day in dull despair, listening for sounds without with an intensity of attention that seemed to pervade every limb, and yet with snatches of sleep that brought dreams more intolerable than the reality which they yet seemed to enhance.

At last, however, the sultry closeness of the day subsided, the Angelus bell sounded far off from the churches and convents of Acre, and near from the chapel tent, and the devotions that it proclaimed were not ended when Richard heard the cry of the crusading watch— "Remember the Holy Sepulchre."

Yes, the Holy Sepulchre might not be recovered and reached by the English army, but it might still be remembered, and therein be laid down all struggles of the will, all rebellious agony, at the being misunderstood, misused, vituperated, all suffering might there be offered up; nor could the most ignominious death stand between him and the thought of that Holy Tomb, and of the joy beyond.—Son of a man who, sorely tried, had drawn his sword against his king, brother of wilful murderers, perhaps to die innocent was the best fate he could hope; and in accordance with the doctrine of his time, he hoped that his death might serve as a part of a sacrifice for the family guilt. Nay, the Prince gone, wherefore should he wish to live?

"Don't you see? The Prince's signet! He said I should bring him! Clown that thou art, hast no eyes nor ears? What, don't you know me? I am the young lord of Dunster, the Prince's foot-page. It is his command."

And amid some perplexed mutterings from the guard, little John of Dunster burst into the tent. "Up, up," he cried, "you are to come to the Prince instantly."

"How fares he?"—Richard's one question of the day.

"Sorely ill at ease," said the boy, "but he wants you, he calls for you, and no one would tell him where you were, so I spoke out at last, and he bade me take his ring and bring you, for 'tis his pleasure. Come now, for the Earl of Lancaster and Hamlyn are gone to take the Princess to Acre, and my Lord of Gloucester has taken his red head off to sleep, and no one is there but old Raymond and some of the grooms.

"The Princess gone!"

"Ay, and Dame Idonea with her. So we shall hear no more of King Coeur de Lion. Hamlyn swears she was on his crusade. Do you think she was, Richard? nobody knows how old she is."

Richard was a great deal too anxious to ask questions himself, to be able to answer this query. And as the yeomen let him pass them, only begging him to bear him out with the Princes, he hastily gathered from the boy all that he could tell. The Prince had, it appeared, been in a most suffering state from pain and fever all the night and the ensuing day, and had hardly noticed any one but his devoted wife, who had attended him unremittingly, until with the cooler air of evening she saw him slightly revived, but was herself so completely spent, and so unwell, as to be incapable of opposing his decision that she should at once be carried into the city to receive the succours her state demanded. When she was gone, Edward, who had perhaps sought to spare her the sight of his last agony, had roused himself to make his will, and choose protectors for his father and young children; and it was after this that his inquiries became urgent for Richard de Montfort. He was at length answered by the indignant little foot-page; and greatly resenting the action of the council, he had, as John said, "frowned and spoken like himself," and sent the little fellow in quest of the young esquire.

The tent was nearly dark, and Richard could only see the outline of the tall form laid prostrate, but the voice he had feared never to hear again, spoke, though slowly and wearily, and a hand was held out. "Welcome, cousin," he said. "Poor boy, they must needs have at thee ere the breath was out of my body; but for that, at least, they shall wait, and longer if my word and will can avail after I am gone. What has given them occasion against thee, Richard?"

"Alas! my Lord, you are too ill at ease to vex yourself with my matters."

"Nay, but I must see thee righted, Richard; there are services for thee to do to me. Hark thee! I have bequeathed thee thy mother's lands at Odiham, which my father gave to me. So mayest thou do for Henry whate'er he will brook," he added, with a languid smile, holding Richard's hand in such a manner as to impress that though his words came very tardily, he did not mean to be interrupted. "Methinks Henry will not grudge a kindly thought and a few prayers for his old comrade. And, Richard, strive to be near my poor boys; strive that they be bred in strict self-rule, and let them hear of the purposes thy father left to me: I think thou knowst them or canst divine them better than any other near me. Thou SHALL be with them if—if Heaven and the blessed Saints bear my sweet wife through this trouble. She will love and trust thee."

Edward's voice broke down in a half-strangled sob between grief and pain; he could not contemplate the thought of his wife, and weakness had broken down much of his power over himself. He did not speak at once, or invite an answer; and when he did, his words were an exclamation of despairing weariness at the trumpet of a gnat that hovered above him.

Richard presently understood that the thin goats' hair curtains which even the crusaders had learnt to adopt from their Oriental neighbours as protections against these enemies, being continually disarranged to give the Prince drink or to put cool applications to his wound, the winged foes were sure to enter, and with their exasperating hum further destroy all chance of rest. The Prince had not slept since he had been wounded, and was well-nigh distraught with wakefulness, and with the continual suffering, which was only diminished at the first moment that a cold lotion touched his arm. The Hospitaliers had sent in some ice from Mount Hermon, but no one knew how to apply it, and even Dame Idonea had despised it.

Fortunately, however, Richard had spent a few weeks on his first arrival in the infirmary of the Knights of St. John, and before his recovery had become familiar with their treatment of both ice and mosquito curtains; and when Edmund of Lancaster came into the tent cautiously in early dawn, he could hardly credit his eyes, for the squire whom he believed to be in close custody was beside his brother, holding the cold applications on the arm, and it was impossible to utter inquiry or remonstrance, for the Prince was in the profoundest, most tranquil slumber.

Nor did he awake till the camp was astir in the morning with the activity that in this summer time could only be exerted before the sun had come to his full strength. Then, when at length he opened his eyes, he pronounced himself to be greatly refreshed; and the physician at the same time found the state of the wound greatly improved. A cheerful answer was returned by the patient to the message of anxious inquiry sent from his Princess at Acre and then looking up kindly at Richard, he said, "Boy, if my wife saved my life once, I think thou hast saved it a second time."

"Brother!" here broke in the Earl of Lancaster, "I would not grieve you, but for your own safety you ought to know of the grave suspicion that has fallen on this youth."

"I know that you all have suspected him from the first, Edmund," returned the Prince coolly, "but I little expected that the first hour of my sickness would be spent in slaking your hatred of him."

"You do not know the reasons, brother," said Edmund, confused; "nor are you in a state to hear them."

"Wherefore not?" said Edward. "Thanks to him, I have my wits clear and cool, and ere the day is older his cause shall be heard. Fetch Gloucester, fetch the rest of the council, and let me hear your witnesses against him! What! do you think I could rest or amend while I know not whether I have a traitor or not beside me?"

There could be no doubt that Edward was fully himself after his night's rest, determined and prompt as ever. No one durst withstand him, and Edmund went to take measures for his being obeyed. Meantime, the Prince grasped Richard by the wrist, and looking him through with the keen blue eyes that seemed capable of piercing any disguise, he said, "Boy, hast thou aught that thou wouldst tell to thy kinsman Edward in this strait, that thou couldst not say to the Prince in council?"

"Sir," said Richard, with choking voice, "I was on my way to give that very warning, when I found that the blow had fallen. My Lord," he added, lowering his tone, as he knelt by the Prince's couch, "Simon lives; I met him on Mount Carmel."

"I thought so," muttered the Prince. "And this is his work?"

Richard hurriedly told the circumstances of the encounter, a matter on which he had the less scruple as Simon was entirely out of reach. He had hardly completed his narration when Prince Edmund returned, and with him came others of the council. Edmund was followed by his squire, Hamlyn; and some of the archers were left without. Richard had told his tale, but had had no assurance of how the Prince would act upon it, nor how far the brand of shame might be made to rest on him and his unhappy house. He had avowed his brother's guilt to the Prince; alas! must it again be blazoned through the camp?

The greetings and inquiries of the new arrivals were hastily got over by the Prince, who lay—holding truly a bed of justice—partly raised by his cushions, with bloodless cheeks indeed, but with flashing eyes, and lips set to all their wonted resoluteness.

"Let me hear, my Lords," he said, "wherefore—so soon as I was disabled—you thought it meet to put mine own body squire and kinsman in ward?"

"Sir," said the Provost Marshal, "these knaves of mine have let an accomplice escape who peradventure might have been made to tell more."

"An accomplice? Of whom?" demanded the Prince.

"Of the—the assassin, my Lord, on whom your own strong hand inflicted chastisement. This Dustifoot, who was the yeoman on guard by your tent, and introduced him to your presence, was seized by the villains at night, endeavouring to hold converse with this gentleman, and was by them taken into custody, whence, I grieve to say, he hath escaped."

"Give his guard due punishment!" said Edward shortly. "But how concerns this the Lord Richard de Montfort's durance?"

"Sir," added the Earl of Gloucester, "is it known to you that the dog of a murderer was yet no Moslem?"

"What of that?" sharply demanded Edward.

"There can scarcely be a doubt," continued the red-haired Earl, "that an attempt on your life, my Lord, could only come from one quarter."

"Oh," dryly replied Edward, "good cause for you to be willing that the Saracen captives should be massacred."

"Sir, I did not then know that the miscreant was not of their faith," said Gloucester. "I now believe that the same revenge that caused the death of Lord Henry of Almayne has now nearly quenched the hope of England, that if you will not be warned, my Lord, worse evil may yet betide."

Gloucester spoke with much feeling, but Edward did not show himself touched; he only said, "All this may be very well, but my question is not answered—Why was my squire put in ward?"

"Speak, Hamlyn," said Edmund of Lancaster; "say to the Prince what thou didst tell me."

Hamlyn stood forth, excusing himself for the painful task of accusing his kinsman, but seeing the Prince's impatient frown, he came to the point, and declared that Richard de Montfort, on meeting him speeding to Acre, had eagerly asked him if aught had befallen the Prince, and had looked startled and confused on being taxed with being aware of what had taken place.

"Well!" said Edward.

Gloucester next beckoned a yeoman forward, who, much confused under the Prince's keen eye, stammered out that he did not wish to harm the young gentleman, but that he had seemed mighty anxious to spare the Pagan hounds of prisoners, and had even been heard to say that their revenge would better fall on himself.

"And is this all for which you had laid hands on him?" said the Prince, looking from one to the other.

"Nay, brother," said Edmund. "It might have been unmarked by thee, but in the first hour myself and others heard him speak of having made speed to warn thee, but finding it too late. Therefore did we conclude that it were well to have him in ward, lest, as in the former unhappy matter, he should have been conversant with traitors, and thus that we might obtain intelligence from him. Remember likewise the fellow who was found in the tent."

"So!" said Edward, "an honourable youth hath been treated as a traitor, because of another springald's opinion of his looks, and because a few yeomen thought he seemed over-anxious to save a few wretched captives, whom they knew to be guiltless. Will there ever come a time when Englishmen will learn what IS witness?"

"His name and lineage, brother," began Edmund.

"That, gentles, is the witness upon which the wolf slew the lamb for fouling the stream."

"Then you will not examine him?" asked Gloucester.

"Not as a suspected felon," said Edward. "One who by your own evidence was heedless of himself in seeking to save the helpless— nay, who spake of hasting to warn me—scarce merits such usage. What consorts with his honour and my safety, I can trust to him to tell me as true friend and liegeman!" and the confiding smile with which he looked at Richard was like a sunbeam in a dark cloud.

"My Lord Prince," objected Gloucester, "we cannot think that this is for your safety."

"See here, Gloucester," said Edward. "Till my arm can keep my head again, double the guards, and search all envoys, under whatever pretext they may enter; but never for the rest of thy life brand a man with imprisonment till you have reasonable proof against him. Thanks for your care of me, my Lords, but I can scarce yet brook long converse. The council is dismissed."

Richard, infinitely relieved, could hardly wait till he could safely speak to the Prince to express his gratitude and joy that he had been not only defended, but freed from all examination, so as to have been spared from denouncing his brother, and that the family had been spared from this additional stigma. Edward, who like all reserved men could not endure the expression of thanks, even while their utter omission would have been wounding, cut him short.

"Tush, boy, Simon is as much my cousin as thy brother, and I would not help to throw fresh stains on the name that, but for my father's selfish counsellors, would stand highest at home! Besides," he added, as one half ashamed of his generosity and willing to qualify it, "supposing it got abroad that he had aimed this stroke at the heir of England—why, then England's honour would be concerned, and we should have stout Gilbert de Clare and all the rest of them wild to storm Simon in his Galilean fastness, without King Herod's boxes, I trow. Then would all the Druses, and the Maronites, and the Saracens, and the half-breeds, the worst of the whole, come down on them in some impassable gorge, and the troops I have taken such pains to keep in health and training would leave their bones in those doleful passes; and not for the sake of the Holy Sepulchre, but of my private quarrel. No, no, Richard, we will keep our own counsel, and do our best that Simon may not get another chance, before I can move within the walls of Acre; and then we will spread our sails, and pray that the Holy Land may make a holier man of him."

CHAPTER XII—THE GARDEN OF THE HOSPITAL

"And who is yon page lying cold at his knee?"—SCOTT.

Edward differed from Coeur de Lion in this, that he was one of the most abstemious men in his army, and disciplined himself at least as rigidly as he did other people. And it was probably on this account that he did not fulfil Dame Idonea's predictions, but recovered favourably, and by the end of a fortnight was able, in the first coolness of early morning, to ride gently into the city of Acre, where a few days previously the Princess Eleanor had given birth to a daughter. She was christened Joan on the day of her father's arrival, and afterwards became the special spoilt favourite of Edward, whose sternness gave place to excessive fondness among his children. Moreover, she in the end became the wife of that same red- haired Earl Gilbert of Gloucester, who at this time stood holding his wax taper, and looking at the small swaddled morsel of royalty with all a bachelor's contempt for infancy, and little dreaming that he beheld his future Countess.

Prince Edward had accepted the invitation of Sir Hugh de Revel, Grand Master of the Order of St. John, to take up his quarters in the Commandery of the brotherhood; and Richard was greatly relieved to have him there, since no watch or ward in the open camp could be so secure as this double fortress, protected in the first place by the walls of the city, and in the second by those of the Hospital itself, with its strict military and monastic discipline.

A wonderful place was that Hospital—infirmary, monastery, and castle, all in one, and with a certain Eastern grace and beauty of its own. The deep massive walls, heavy towers, and portcullised gateway, were in the most elaborate and majestic style of defensive architecture; and the main building rose to a great height, filled with galleries of small, bare, rigid-looking cells, just large enough for a knight, his pallet, and his armour. Below was a noble vaulted hall, the walls hung with well-tried hawberks, and shields and helmets which had stood many a dint; captured crescents and green banners waved as trophies over crooked scymetars and Damascus blades inlaid with sentences from the Koran in gold, and twisted cuirasses rich with barbaric gold and gems; the blazoned arms of the noblest families of France, Spain, England, Germany, and Italy, decked the panels and brightened the windows; while the stone pulpit for the reader showed that it was still a convent refectory.

The chapel was grave and massive, but at the same time gorgeous with colouring suited to eyes accustomed to Oriental brightness of hue; the chancel walls were inlaid with the porphyry, jasper, and marble, of exquisite tints, that came from the mountains around; the shrines were touched with gold, and the roofs and vaultings painted with fretwork of unapproachable brilliance and purity of tints; yet all harmonizing together, as only Eastern colouring can harmonize, and giving a sense of rest and coolness.

Within those huge thick walls, whose windows, sunk deep into their solid mass, only let in threads of jewelled light, under their solemn circular richly carved brows, between those marble pillars; the elder ones, round and solid, with Romanesque mighty strength; the new graceful clusters of shining blood-red marble shafts, surrounding a slender white one, all banded together with gold, under the vaults of the stone roof, upon the mosaic floor—there was always a still refreshing coolness, like the "shadow of a great rock in a weary land." One transept had a window communicating with the upper room of the Infirmary, so that the sick who there lay in their beds might take part in the services in the chapel.

The outer court, with the great fortified gateway towards the street, was a tilt-yard, where martial exercises took place as in any other castle; but pass through the great hall to the inner court, of which the chapel formed one side, and where could such cloisters have been found in the West? Their heavy columns and deep-browed arches clinging against the thick walls, afforded unfailing shelter from the sun, and their coolness was increased by the marble of the pavement, inlaid in rich intricate mosaics.

Extending around the interior of the external wall, they enclosed an exquisite Eastern garden, perfumed with flowering shrubs, shady with trees, and lovely with tall white lilies, hollyhocks, purple irises, stars of Bethlehem, and many another Eastern flower, which would send forth seeds or roots for the supply of the trim gardens of Western convents. The soft bubbling of fountains gave a sense of delicious freshness; doves flew hither and thither, and their soft murmuring was heard in the branches; and at certain openings in their foliage might be seen the azure of the Mediterranean, which little John of Dunster persisted in calling too blue—why could it not be a sober proper-coloured sea like his own Bristol Channel?

Richard was very happy here. There was something of the same charm as in modern days is experienced in staying at a college. The brethren were thorough monks in religious observance, but they were also high-bred nobles, and had seen many wild adventures, and hard- fought battles, and moreover, had entertained in turn almost every variety of pilgrim who had visited the Holy Land; so that none could have been found who had more of interest to tell, or more friendly hospitable kindness towards their guests. Richard was a favourite there, not only as a friend of Reginald Ferrers, but as acquainted with the Grand Prior, Sir Robert Darcy, whose memory was still green in Palestine. Tales of his feats of mighty strength still lingered at Acre; how he had held together, by his single arm, the gates of a house in the retreat from

Damietta, against a whole troop of Mamelukes, until every Christian had left it on the other side, and then had slowly followed them, not a Moslem daring to attack him; how he had borne off wounded knights on his back, and on sultry marches would load himself with the armour of any one who was exhausted, and never fail to declare it was exactly what he liked best! More than once it had been intimated that Richard de Montfort would be gladly accepted as a brother of the Order; and he often thought over the offer, but not only was he unwilling to separate himself from the Prince, but he felt it needful at any rate to return to England to judge of the condition of his brother Henry, ere becoming one of an Order where he could no longer dispose of himself.

He was resolved never to quit the Prince till he had seen him beyond the reach of any machination of his brother's, nor indeed was it easy to think of parting at all, for Edward, who had relaxed all coldness of manner towards him ever since the affair at Trapani, had now become warmly affectionate and confidential. The Prince was still far from having regained his usual health, his arm was still in a scarf, and was often painful, and the least exposure to the sun brought on violent headache, which some attributed to the poison in the scratch on his forehead, but the Hospitaliers, more reasonably, ascribed to a slight sun-stroke. Their character of infirmarers rendered them especially considerate hosts, and they never overwhelmed their guest with the stiff formalities of courtesy for his rank's sake, but allowed him to follow his inclination, and this led him to spend great part of his time in a pavilion, a thoroughly Eastern erection, which stood in the garden, at the top of the white marble steps leading to a fountain of delicious sparkling water, and sheltered from the sun by the dark solid horizontal branches of a noble Cedar of Lebanon, which tradition connected with the visit of the Empress Helena. Here, lying upon mats placed on the steps, the convalescent Prince would rest for hours, sometimes holding converse with the Grand Master, or counsel with his visitors from the camp; but more often in the dreamy repose of recovery, silent or talking to Richard of matters that lay deep within his heart; but which, perhaps, nothing but this softening species of waking dream would have drawn from him. He would dwell on those two hero models of his boyhood, so diverse, yet so closely connected together by their influence upon his character, Louis of France, and Simon of Leicester; and of the impression both had left, that judgment, mercy, faith, and the subject's welfare, were the primary duties of a sovereign—an idea only now and then glimpsed by the feudal sovereigns, who thought that the people lived for them rather than they for the people. And when, as in England, the King's good-nature had been abused by swarms of foreign-born relations, who had not even his claims on the people, no wonder the yoke had been galling beyond endurance. Of the end Edward could not bear to think—of the broken friendships—the enmity of kindred—the faults on either side that had embittered the strife, till he had been forced to become the sword in the hands of the royal party to liberate his father—and with consequences that had so far out-run his powers of controlling them. To make England the land of law, peace, and order, that Simon de Montfort would fain have seen it, was his present aspiration; and then, he said, when all was purified at home, it might yet be permitted to him to return and win back the Holy City, Jerusalem, to the Christian world. In the meantime, as a memorial of this, his earnest longing, he was causing, at great expense and labour, one of the huge stones of the Temple to be transported over the hills, and embarked on board a ship, to carry home with him. Richard, meantime, learnt to know and love his Prince with a more devoted love, if that were possible, and to grieve the more at the persistent hatred of his brothers, who, utterly uncomprehending their father's high purposes themselves, sought blindly to slake their vengeance for the ruin they had themselves provoked, and upon one who mourned him far more truly than they could ever do.

A few days had thus passed, when Richard was one day called by his friend, Sir Raynald, into the Infirmary, to speak a few kind words to a dying English pilgrim, who had come from his native country, and confided to him his dearly-purchased palm and scallop shell, to be conveyed to his aged mother.

As Richard was passing along the great lofty chamber, two rows of beds were arranged; one of the patients rather hastily, as it seemed to him, enveloped himself in his coverlet, leaving nothing visible but a great black patch which seemed to cover the whole side of his face.

"That is a strange varlet," said Raynald, as they passed him; "it is an old wound that the patch covers, not what has brought him here; and what the nature of his ailment may be, not one of our infirmarers can make out; his tongue is purple, and he hath such strange shiverings and contortions in all his limbs, that they are at their wits' end, and some hold that he must have undergone some sorcery in his passage through the Infidel domains."

"He came from the East, then?" asked Richard.

"Yea, verily. We have many more sick among the returning than the out-going pilgrims."

"And what is his nation?"

"Nay; all the scanty words he hath spoken have been in Lingua Franca, and he hath been in such trances and trembling fits that it hath not been easy to question him. Nor is it our custom to trouble a pilgrim with inquiries."

"How did he enter?" said Richard.

"Brother Antonio found him yester-eve cast down, gasping for breath, by the gate of the Hospital, just able to entreat for the love of St. John to be admitted. He had all the tokens of a pilgrim about him, and seemed better at first, walked lustily to bath and bed, and did not show himself helpless; but I much suspect his disease is the work of the Arch Enemy, for he is always at his worst if one of our Brethren in full orders comes near him. You saw how he cowered and hid himself when I did but pass through the hall. I shall speak to the Preceptor, and see if it were not best to try what exorcism will do."

There was something in all this that made Richard vaguely uneasy. After the recent attack upon the Prince, he suspected all that he did not fully understand; and though in the guarded precincts of the Hospital he had once dismissed his anxiety, it returned upon him in redoubled force. He thought of Nick Dustifoot, but that worthy was of a uniform tint of whitey brown, skin, hair and all; and Richard had assured himself that the strange patient had black hair and a brown skin, but that was all that he could guess at. The exorcism would, however, be an effectual means of disclosing the "myster wight's" person, and it sometimes included measures so strong, that few pretences could hold out against them. But it was too serious and complicated a ceremony to be got up at short notice; and when they met in the Refectory for supper, Raynald told Richard that the Grand Master intended to make a personal inspection next day, before deciding on using his spiritual weapons.

"And then!" cried John of Dunster, dancing round, "you will let me be there! Pray, good Father, let me be there! Oh, I hope there will be a rare smell of brimstone, and the foul fiend will come out with huge claws, and a forked tail. I don't care to see him if he only comes out like a black crow; I can see crows enough in the trees at Dunster."

"Peace, John; this is no place for idle talk," said Richard gravely. "Stand aside, here comes the Prince."

The Prince had spent a fatiguing day over the terms of the ten years, ten months, ten weeks, ten days, ten hours, and ten minutes' truce with the Emir of Joppa; he ate little, and after the meal, took Richard's arm, and craved leave from the Grand Master to seek the fresh air beneath the cedar tree. And when there, he could not endure the return to the closeness of his own apartment, but declared his intention of sleeping in the pavilion. He dismissed his attendants, saying he needed no one but Richard, who, since his illness, had always slept upon cushions at his feet.

Where was Richard?

He presently appeared, carrying on one arm a mantle, and over the other shoulder the Prince's immense two-handled sword; while his own sword was in his belt. Leonillo followed him.

"How now!" said Edward, "are we to have a joust? Dost look for phantom Saracens out of yonder fountain, such as my Dona tells me rise out of the fair wells in Castille, wring their hands and pray for baptism?"

"You said your hand should keep your head, my Lord," said Richard; "this is but a lone place."

"What! amid all the guards of the good Fathers! Well, old comrade," as he took his sword in his right hand; "I am glad to handle thee once more, and I hope soon to grasp thee as I am wont, with both hands. Lay it down, Richard. There—thanks—that is well. I wonder what my father would have thought if one of his many crusading vows had led him hither. Should we ever have had him back again? How well this dreamy leisure would have suited him! It would almost make a troubadour of a rough warrior like me. See the towers and pinnacles against the sky, and the lights within the windows—and the stars above like lamps of gold, and the moonshine sparkling on the bubbles of the water, ever floating off, yet ever in the same place. Were the good old man here, how peacefully would he sing, and pray, and dream, free from debts, parliament and barons. Ah! had his kinsmen let him keep his vow, it had been happier for us all."

So mused the Prince, and with a weary smile resigned himself to rest.

But Richard was too full of vague uneasiness to sleep. He could not dismiss from his mind the thought of the unknown pilgrim, and was resolved to relax no point of vigilance until the full investigation should have satisfied him that his fears were unfounded. He had been accustomed to watching and broken rest during the Prince's illness, and though he durst not pace up and down for fear of disturbing the sleeper—nay, could hardly venture a movement—he strained his eyes into the twilight, and told his beads fervently; but sleep hung on him like a spell, and even while sitting upright there were strange dreams before him, and one that he had had before, though with a variation. It was the field of Evesham once more; but this time the strange pilgrim rose in his dark wrappings before him, and suddenly developed into that same shadowy form of his father, who again struck him on the shoulder with his sword, and dubbed him again "The Knight of Death."

Hark! there was a growl from Leonillo; a footstep, a dark figure—the pilgrim himself! Richard shouted aloud, grasped at his sword, and flung himself forward.

"Montfort's vengeance!" The sound rang in his ears as a sharp pang thrilled through his side; the hot blood welled up, and he was dashed to the ground;

but even in falling he heard the Prince's "What treason is this?" and felt the rising of the mighty form. At the same moment the murderer was in the grasp of that strong right hand, and was dragged forward into the full light of the lamp that hung from the roof of the pavilion.

"Thou!" he gasped. "Who—what?"

"Richard!" exclaimed the Prince, and relaxing his hold, "Simon de Montfort, thou hast slain thy brother!"

The sudden shock and awe had overwhelmed Simon, who was indeed weaponless, since his dagger remained in Richard's wound. He silently assisted the Prince in lifting Richard to the cushions of the couch, and the low groan convinced them that he lived: looked anxiously for the wound. The dagger had gone deep between the ribs, and little but the haft could be seen.

"Poisoned?" Edward asked, looking up at Simon.

"No. It failed once. He may live," said Simon, with bent brows and folded arms.

"No, no. My death-blow!" gasped Richard, with sobbing breath. "Best so, if —Oh, could I but speak!"

The Prince raised him, supporting his head on his own broad breast and shoulder, and signed to Simon to hold to his lips the cup of water that stood near. Richard slightly revived, and in this posture breathed more easily.

"He might yet live. Call speedy aid!" said the Prince, who seemed to have utterly forgotten that he was practically alone with his persevering and desperate enemy.

"Wait! Oh, wait!" cried Richard, holding out his hand; "it would be vain; but it will be all joy did I but know that there will be no more of this. Simon, he loved my father—he has spared thee again and again."

"Simon," said the Prince, "for this dear youth's sake and thy father's, I raise no hand against thee. Bitter wrong has been done to thy house, by what persons, and how provoked, it skills not now to ask. Twice thy fury has fallen on the guiltless. Enough blood has been shed. Let there be peace henceforth."

Simon stood moody, with folded arms, and Richard groaned, and essayed to speak.

"Peace, boy," tenderly said Edward; "and thou, Simon, hear me. I loved thy father, and knew the upright noble spirit that arrayed him against us. Heaven is my witness that I would have given my life to have been able to save him on yon wretched battle-field. But he fell in fair fight, in helm and corselet, like a good knight. Peace be with him! Surely in this land of pardon and redemption his son and nephew may cease to seek one another's blood for his sake! Cheer thy brother by letting him feel his brave deed hath not been fruitless. Free thou shalt go—do what thou wilt; no word of mine shall betray that this deed is thine."

"Lay aside thy purpose," entreated Richard. "Bind him by oath, my Lord."

"Nay," said the Prince. "Here, on foreign soil, the strife lies between the cousins, the sons of Henry and of Eleanor; and if Simon must needs still slake his revenge in my blood, he may have better success another time. Or, so soon as I can wear my armour again, I offer him a fair combat in the lists, man to man; better so than staining his soul with privy murder—but I had far rather that it should be peace between us—and that thou shouldst see it." And Edward, still supporting Richard on his breast, held out his right hand to Simon, adding, "Let not thy brother's blood be shed in vain."

Richard made a gesture of agonized entreaty.

"My father—my father!" he said. "He forgave—he hated blood; Simon, didst but know—"

"I see," said Simon impatiently, "that Heaven and earth alike are set against my purpose. Fear not for his days, Richard, they are safe from me, and here is my hand upon it."

The tone was sullen and grudging, and Richard looked scarcely comforted; but the Prince was in haste that he should be succoured at once, and even while receiving Simon's unwilling hand, said, "We lose time. Speed near enough to the Spital to be heard, and shout for aid. Then seek thine own safety. I will say no more of thy share in this matter."

Simon lingered one moment. "Boy," he said, "I told thee thou wast over like him. Live, live if thou canst! Alas! I had thought to make surer work this time; but thou dost pardon me the mischance?"

"More than pardon—thank thee—since he is safe," whispered Richard, and as Simon bent over him the boy crossed his brow, and returned a look of absolute joy.

Simon sped away; and the Prince, when left alone with Richard, put no restraint upon the warmth of his feelings, and his tears fell fast and freely.

"Boy, boy," he said; "I little thought thou wast to bear what was meant for me!" And then, with tenderness that would have seemed foreign to his nature, he inquired into the pain that Richard was suffering, tried to make his position more easy, and lamented that he could not venture to draw out the weapon until the leeches should come.

"It has been my best hope," said Richard; "and now that it should have been thus. With your goodness I have nothing—nothing to wish. Sir Raynald will be here—I have only my charge for Henry to give him—and poor Leonillo!"

"I will bear thy charges to Henry," said the Prince. "Nor shall he think thou didst betray his secret. I will watch over him so far as he will let me, and do all I may for his child. Yet it may be thou wilt still return. I hear the stir in the House. They will be here anon. Thou must live, Richard, my friend, where I have few friends. I thought to have knighted thee, boy, when thou hadst won fame. Oh, would that I had shown thee more of my love while it was time!"

"All, all I hoped or longed for I have," murmured Richard. "If you see Henry, my Lord, bear him my greetings—and to poor Adam—yea, and my mother. Oh! would that I could make them all know your kindness and my joy—that it should be thus!"

By this time the whole Hospital was astir, and the knights and lay brethren came flocking out in consternation and dread of finding their royal host himself murdered within their cloisters.

Great was the confusion, and eager the search for the assassin, while others crowded round the Prince, who still would not give up his post of supporting the sufferer in his arms, while a few moments' examination convinced the experienced infirmarers that the wound was mortal, and that the extraction of the dagger would but hasten death, which could not be other than very near. Indeed, Richard already spoke with such difficulty that only the Prince's ear could detect his entreaty that Raynald Ferrers might act as his priest. Raynald was already near, only withheld by the crowd of knights of higher degree who had thronged before him. Richard looked up to him with a face that in all its mortal agony seemed to ask congratulation. The power of making confession was gone, and when Raynald would have offered to take him in his own arms, both he and the Prince showed disinclination to the move. So thus they still remained, while the young knightly priest spoke the words of Absolution, and then, across the solemn darkness of the garden, amid the light of tapers, the Host was borne from the Chapel, while the low subdued chant of the brethren swelled up through the night air. Poor little John of Dunster, with his arms round Leonillo's neck, to keep him from disturbing his master, knelt, sobbing as though his heart would break, but trying to stifle the sounds as the priest's voice came grave and full on the silent air, responded to by the gathered tones of the brethren: the fountain bubbled on, and the wakening birds began to stir in the trees.

Once more Richard opened his eyes, looked up at his Prince, and smiled. That smile remained while Edward kissed his brow with fervour, laid him down on the cushions, and rising to his feet, bowed his head to the Grand Master, but did not even strive to speak, and gravely walked across the cloister, with a slow though steady step, to his own chamber. No one saw him again till the sun was high, when, with looks as composed as ever, he went forth to lay his page's head in the grave, and thence visit and calm the fears of his Princess.

Search had everywhere been made for the assassin, but no traces of him were found. Only the strange pilgrim had vanished in the confusion; and the Prince never contradicted the Grand Master in his indignation that a Moslem hound should have assumed such a disguise.

CHAPTER XIII—THE BEGGAR AND THE PRINCE

"This favour only, that thou would'st stand out of my sunshine."
DIOGENES.

It was the last week of August, 1274, the morrow of the most splendid coronation that England had ever beheld, either for the personal qualities and appearance of the sovereigns, or for the magnificence of the adornments, and the bounteous feasting of multitudes.

A whole fortnight of entertainments to rich and poor had been somewhat exhausting, even to the guests; and the suburbs of London wore an unusually sleepy and quiescent appearance in the hot beams of the August sun. Bethnal Green lay very silent, parched, and weary, not even enlivened by its usual gabbling flocks of geese, all of whom, poor things! except the patriarchal gander, and one or two of his ladies, had gone to the festival—but to return no more!

One of those who had been in the midst of the pageant, and had returned unscathed, was Blind Hal of Bethnal Green. Many a coin had gone into his scrip—uncontested king of the beggars as he was; many a savoury morsel had been conveyed to him and his child by his admiring brethren of the wallet; with many a gibing scoff had he driven from the field presuming mendicants, not of his own fraternity; and with half-bitter, half-amused remarks, had he listened to the rapturous descriptions of the splendours of king, queen, and their noble suite. And pretty Bessee had clung fast to his hand, and discreetly guided him through every maze of the crowd, with the strange dexterity of a child bred up in throngs. And now tired out with the long-continued festivities, the beggar sat in front of his hut, basking in the sun, and more than half asleep; while Bessee, her lap full of heather-blossoms and long bents of grass, was endeavouring to weave herself chains, bracelets, and coronals, in imitation of those which had recently dazzled her eyes.

She had just encircled her dark auburn locks with a garland of purple heather, studded here and there with white or gold, when, starting upon her little bare but delicately clean pink feet, she laid her hand on her father's lap, and said, "Father, hark! I see two of the good red monks coming!"

"Well, child; and wherefore waken me? They are after their own affairs, I trow. Moreover, I hear no horses' feet."

"They are not riding," said Bessee; "and they are walking this way. They have a dog, too! Oh, such a gallant glorious dog, father! Ah," cried she joyfully, "'tis the good Father Grand Prior!" and she was about to start forward, but the blind man's ear could now distinguish the foot-falls; and holding her fast, he almost gasped—"And the other, child—who is he?"

"No knight at our Spital! A stranger, father. So tall, so tall!
His mantle hardly reaches his knee his robe leaves his ankles bare.
O father, they are coming. Let me go to meet dear good Father
Robert! But what—Oh, is the fit coming? Father Robert will stop it!"

"Hush thy prattle," said the beggar, clutching her fast, and listening as one all ear; and by this time the two knights were close at hand, the taller holding the dog, straining in a leash, while the good Grand Prior spoke. "How fares it with thee, friend? And thou, my pretty one? No mishaps among the throng?"

"None," returned Hal; "though the King and his suite DID let loose five hundred chargers in the crowd at their dismounting, to trample down helpless folk, and be caught by rogues. Largesse they called it! Fair and convenient largesse—easily providing for those that received it!"

"No harm was done," briefly but sharply exclaimed the strange knight; and the blind man, who had, as little Bessee at least perceived, been turning his acute ear in that direction all the time he had been speaking, now let his features light up with sudden perception.

But Sir Robert Darcy, thinking that he only now became aware of the stranger's presence, said, "A knight is here from the East, who brings thee tidings, my son."

Sir Robert would have said more, but the beggar standing up, cut him short, by saying, "So, cousin, you have yet to learn the vanity of disguises and feignings towards a blind man."

"Nay, fair cousin," was the answer, "my feigning was not towards you; but I doubted me whether you would have the world see me visit you in my proper character. Will not you give me a hand, Henry?"

"First say to me," said Henry, embracing with his maimed arm his staff, planted in front of him defiantly, and still holding tight his little daughter in his hand, "what brings you here to break into the peace of the poor remnant of a man you have left?"

"I come," said Edward patiently, "to fulfil my last—my parting promise, to one who loved us both—and gave his life for me."

"Loved you, ay! and well enough to betray me to you!" said Henry bitterly.

"No, Henry de Montfort, ten thousand times no!" said Edward. "I would maintain in the lists the honour and loyalty of my Richard towards you and me and all others. His faithfulness to you brought him into peril of death and disgrace in the wretched matter of poor Henry of Almayne; and he would have met both rather than have broken his faith."

"Then," said Henry, still with the same mocking tone, "how was it that my worthless existence became known to his Grace?"

"I knew of your having vanished from Evesham Abbey," returned Edward: "and thus knowing, I understood a letter, the writing of which had brought suspicion on Richard, and which was brought back to me when we were seeking into—"

"Into the deed of Simon and Guy," said Henry. "Poor Henry! It was a foul crime; and Father Robert can bear me witness that I did penance for it, when that kindly heart of his was laid in St. Peter's Abbey."

"Then, Henry, thou own'st thy kinship to us still," said Edward earnestly. Give me thine hand, man, and let me embrace my lovely little kinswoman—a queen in her trappings. Ah, Henry! Heaven hath dealt lovingly with thee in sparing thee thy child!"

"You have children left!" said Henry quickly, and not withholding a hand— which, be it remarked, was as delicately shaped and well kept as that which took it.

Twice had the beggar received a dole at Westminster at the obsequies of Edward's little sons; yea, though he and all his brethren of the dish had all the winter before had alms given them to purchase their prayers for the health of the last.

"Three—but three out of six," answered Edward; "nor dare I reckon on the life of the frail babe that England hailed yesterday as my heir. I sometimes deem that the blight of broken covenants has fallen on my sons."

"They were none of your breaking," said Henry.

"Say'st thou so!" exclaimed Edward, looking up, with the animation of a man hearing an acquittal from a quarter whose sincerity he could thoroughly trust.

But Henry made no courtly answer. "Pshaw! no living man that had to deal with or for your father could keep a covenant. You were but the spear-point of the broken reed, good cousin; and we pitied and excused you accordingly."

"Your father did," said Edward hoarsely. He could brook pity from the great Simon better than from the blind beggar.

"Ay, marry, that did he," returned Henry, "as he closed his visor that last morn, after looking out on that wild Welsh border scum that my fair brother-in-law had marshalled against us. 'By the arm of St. James,' said he, 'if Edward take not heed, that rascaille will deal with us in a way that will be worse for him than for us!'"

"A true foreboding," said the King. "Henry, do thou come and be with me. All are gone! Scarce a face that I left in England has welcomed me on my return. Come, thou, in what guise thou wilt—earl, counsellor, or bedesman—only be with me, and speak to me thy father's words."

"Who—I, my Lord?" returned Henry. "I am no man to speak my father's words! They flew high over my head, and were only caught by grave youths such as yourself. I, who was never trusted with so much as a convoy. No, no; all the counsel I shall ever give, is to the beggars, which coat-of-arms is like to rain clipped silver, and which honest round penny pieces! Poor Richard! he bore the best brain of us all, and might have served your purpose. Sit down, and tell me of the lad.—Bessee, little one, bring out the joint-stool for the holy Father."

And Henry de Montfort made way on the rude bench outside his hut, with all the ease and courtesy of the Earl of Leicester receiving his kinsman the King. But meantime, the dog, which had been straining in the leash, held by Edward throughout the conference, leapt forward, and vehemently solicited the beggar's caresses. "Ah, Leonillo!" he said, recognizing him at once, "thou hast lost thy master! Poor dog! thou art the one truly loyal to thy master's blood!"

"It was Richard's charge to take him to thee," said Edward: "but if he be burdensome to thee, I would gladly cherish him, or would commit him to faithful Gourdon, with whom he might be happier. Since he lost his master the poor hound hath much pined away, and will take food from none but me, or little John of Dunster."

Leonillo, however, who seemed to have an unfailing instinct for a Montfort, was willingly accepting the eager and delighted attentions of the little girl; though he preferred those of her father, and cowered down beneath his hand, with depressed ears and gently waving tail, as though there were something in the touch and voice that conferred what was as near bliss as the faithful creature could enjoy without his deity and master.

Meantime, the Grand Prior discreetly removed his joint-stool out of hearing of the two cousins, and called the little maid to rehearse to him the Credo and Ave, with their English equivalents—a task that pretty Bessee highly disapproved after the fortnight's dissipation, and would hardly have performed for one less beloved of children than Father Robert.

The good Grand Prior knew that the King would have much to say that would beseem no ear save his kinsman's; and in effect Edward told what none besides would ever hear respecting the true author of the attempts on his own life.

"Spiteful fox. Such Simon ever was!" was the beggar's muttered comment. "Well that he knows not of my poor child! So, cousin, thou hast kept his counsel," he added in a different tone. "I thank thee in the name of Montfort and Leicester. It was well and nobly done."

And Henry de Montfort held out his hand with the dignity of head of the family whose honour Edward had shielded.

"It was for thy father's sake and Richard's," said Edward, receiving the acknowledgment as it was meant.

"Ah, well," said Henry, relapsing into his usual half-scoffing tone; "in that boy our Montfort blood seems to have run clear of the taint it got from the she-fiend of Anjou."

"Thy share was from a mocking fiend!" returned the King.

"Ay, and a fair portion it is!" said the beggar. "My jest and my song have borne me through more than my sword and spurs ever did—and have been more to me than English earldom or French county. Poor Richard!" he added with feeling; "I told him his was the bondage and mine the freedom!"

"Alas! I fear that so it was," said Edward. "My favour only embittered his foes. Had I known how it would end, I had never taken him to me; but my heart yearned to my uncle's goodly son."

"Maybe it is well," said Henry. "Had the boy grown up verily like my father, thou and he might have fallen out; or if not—why, you knights and nobles ride in miry bloody ways, and 'tis a wonder if even the best of you does not bring his harness home befouled and besmirched—not as shining bright as he took it out. Well, what didst thou with the poor lad? Cut him in fragments? You mince your best loved now as fine as if they were traitors."

"No," said Edward; "the boy lies sleeping in the Church of St. John, at Acre. I rose from my sickbed that I might lay him in his grave as a brother. Lights burn round him, and masses are said; and the brethren were left in charge to place his effigy on his tomb, in carven stone. One day I trust to see it. My brother Alexander of Scotland, Llewellyn of Wales, and I, have sworn to one another to bring all within these four seas into concord and good order; and then we may look for such a blessing on our united arms as may bear us onward to Jerusalem! Then come with us, Henry, and let us pray together at Richard's grave."

"I may safely promise," said Henry, smiling, "if this same Crusade is to be when peace and order are within the four seas. Moreover, thou wilt have ruined my trade by that time!"

"Nay, Henry, cease fooling. See—if thou wilt not be thyself, I will find thee a lodge in any park of mine. None shall know who thou art; but thou shalt have free range, and—"

"And weary of my life! No, no, cousin. I am in thy power now; and thou canst throw me into prison as the attainted Lord de Montfort. Do so if thou wilt; but I were fooling indeed to give up my free range, my power, my authority, to be a poor suspected, pitied, maimed pensioner on thy bounty. Park, quotha! with none to speak to from morn to night. I can have my will of any park of thine I please, whenever I choose!"

Edward would have persisted, but Henry silenced him effectually, with a sarcastic hint that his favours had done little for Richard. Then the King prayed at least that he would consider his child; but to the proposal of taking her to the palace, Henry returned an indignant negative: "He had seen enough of the court ladies," he said.

A hot glow of anger lighted Edward's cheek, for he loved his mother; but the blind beggar could not be the subject of his wrath, and he merely said, "Thou didst not know my wife!"

"Ay, I will believe the court as perfect as thou thinkest to make the isle; but Bessee shall not bide there. She is the blind beggar's child, and such shall she remain. Send me to a dungeon, as I said, and thou canst pen her in a convent, or make her a menial to thy princesses, as thou wilt; but while my life and my freedom are my own I keep my child."

"I could find it in my heart to arrest thee," said Edward, "when I look at that beautiful child, and think to what thou wouldst bring her."

"She is fair then," said the beggar eagerly.

"Fair! She is the loveliest child mine eyes have looked on: though some of mine own have been very lovely. But she hath the very features of our royal line—though with eyes deep and dark, like thy father's, or my Richard's—and a dark glow of sunny health on her fair skin. She bears her, too, right royally. Henry, thou canst not wreck the fate of a child like that."

"No, assuredly," said Henry dryly. "I have not done so ill by her hitherto, by thine own showing, that I should not be trusted with her for the future."

"The parting would be bitter," began Edward "but thou shouldst see her often."

"Slay me, and make her a ward of the crown," said Henry. "Otherwise I will need no man's leave for seeing my daughter. But ask her. If she will go with thee, I will say no more."

King Edward was fond of children—most indulgent to his own, and kind to all little ones, who, attracted by the sweetness which his stern, grave, beautiful countenance would assume when he looked at them— always made friends with him readily. So he trusted to this fascination in the case of the little Lady Elizabeth. He held out his hands to her, and claimed her as his cousin; and she came readily to him, and stood between his knees. "Little cousin, he said, "wilt thou come home with me, to be with my two little maids, the elder much of thine age?"

"You are a red monk!" said Bessee, amazed.

"That's his shell, Bessee," said her father; "he has come a-masking, and forgot his part."

"I don't like masking," said Bessee, trying to get away.

"Then we will mask no more," said Edward. "Thou hast looked in my face long enough with those great black eyes. Dost know me, child?"

Bessee cast the black eyes down, and coloured.

"Dost know me?" he repeated.

"I think," she whispered at last, "that you are masking still. You are like—like the King that was crowned at the Abbey."

"Well said, little maid! And shall I take thee home, and give thee pearls and emeralds to braid thy locks, instead of these heath- bells?"

"Father," said Bessee, trying to withdraw her little hands out of Edward's large one, which held both fast. "O father, is he masking still?"

"No, child; it is the King indeed," said Henry. "Hear what he saith to thee."

And again Edward spoke of all that would tempt a child.

"Father," said Bessee, "if father comes!"

"No, Bessee," said her father; "I have done with palaces. No places they for blind beggars."

"Oh, let me go! let me go!" cried Bessee, struggling. And as the King released her hands, she flew to her father. "He would lose himself without me! I must be with father. O King, go away! Father, don't let him take me! Let me cry for Jock of the Wooden Spoon, and Trig One Leg, and Hedgerow Wat!"

"Hush, hush, Bess!" said Henry, not desirous that his royal cousin should understand the strength of his body-guard of honour. "The King here is as trusty and loyal as the boldest beggar among us. He only gave thee thy choice between him and me!"

"Thee, thee, father. He can't want me. He has two eyes and two hands, and a queen and two little girls; and thou hast only me!" and she clung round her father's neck.

"Little one," said Edward, "thou need'st not shrink from me. I will not take thee away. Thy father hath a treasure, and 'tis his part to strive not to throw it away. Only should either thou or he ever condescend so far as to seek for counsel with this poor cousin of thine, send this token to me, and I will be with thee."

But it was full nine years ere Edward saw that jewel again. Meantime he was not entirely without knowledge of his kinsman. On every great occasion the figure, conspicuous for the scrupulous cleanliness of the dark russet gown, and the careful arrangement of the hair and beard, and the fillet which covered the eyes, as well as for a lordly bearing, that even the stoop of blindness could not disguise, was to be seen dominating over all the other beggars, sitting on the steps of church or palace gates, as if they had been a throne; troubling himself little to beg, but exchanging shrewd remarks with all who addressed him, and raising many a laugh among the bystanders. Leonillo lay contented at his feet; but after just enough time had elapsed to show that he cared not for the King's remonstrance, he ceased to be accompanied by his little daughter, and was led by a boy in her stead.

The King, making inquiries of the Grand Prior, learnt that pretty Bessee was daily deposited at the sisterhood of Poor Clares, where she remained while her father was out on his begging expeditions, and learnt such breeding as convents then gave.

"In sooth," said Sir Robert, "honest Hal believes it is all for good- will and charity and love to the pretty little wench; and so it is in great part: but methought it best to give a hint to the mother prioress that the child came of good blood. She is a discreet lady, and knows how to deal with her; and truly she tells me their house has prospered since the little one came to them. Every feast-day morn have they found their alms-dish weightier with coin than ever she knew it before."

When Edward repeated this intelligence to his queen, she recollected Dame Idonea's gossiping information—that brave Sir Robert, the flower of the House of Darcy, had only entered the Order of St. John, when fair Alda Braithwayte, in the strong enthusiasm of the Franciscan preaching, had pleaded a vow of virginity against all suitors, and had finally become a Sister of the Poor Clares. And after all his wars and wanderings, the regulations of his Order had ended by bringing the Hospitalier in his old age into the immediate neighbourhood of Prioress Alda; and into that distant business intercourse that the heads of religious houses had from time to time to carry on together.

The world passed on. Eleanor de Montfort came from France, and the King himself acted the part of a father to her at her marriage with Llewellyn of Wales. He knew—though she little guessed—that the beggar, by whom her jewelled train swept with rustling sound, was the first-born of her father's house, and should have held her hand. Two years only did that marriage last; Eleanor died, leaving an infant daughter; and Llewellyn soon after was in arms against the English. Perhaps Edward bethought him of his cousin's ironical promise to go with him to the East after the pacification of the whole island, when he found himself obliged to summon the fierce Pyrenean to pursue the wild Welsh in their mountains.

CHAPTER XIV—THE QUEEN OF THE DEW-DROPS

"This is the prettiest low-born lass that ever
Ran on a green sward." —Winter's Tale.

It was the summer of 1283; the babe of Carnarvon had been accepted as the native prince, speaking no tongue but Welsh, and Edward had since been employed in establishing his dominion over Wales. His Whitsuntide was kept by the Queen's special entreaty at St. Winifred's Well. Such wonders had been told her of the miracles wrought by this favourite Welsh saint, that she hoped that by early placing her little Welsh-born son under such protection, she might secure for him healthier and longer life than had been the share of his brethren.

So to Holy-well went the court and army. Some lodged in the convent attached to the well; but many and many more dwelt in tents, or lodged in cottages, or raised huts of boughs of trees. Noble ladies of Eleanor's suite were glad to obtain a lodging in rude Welsh huts; and as the weather was beautiful, there was plenty of gay feasting, dancing, and jousting on the greensward, when the religious observances of the day were over. Pilgrims thronged from all parts, attracted both by the presence of the court and the unusual tranquillity of Wales; and for nearly a mile around the Holy-well it was like one great motley fair, resorted to by persons of all stations. Beggars of course were there in numbers, and among them the unfailing blind beggar of Bethnal Green, who always made a pilgrimage in the summer to some station of easy access from London, but whom some wondered to see at such a distance.

"Had he scented that the court was coming?" asked the young nobles.

"Not he; he never haunted courts. He would have kept away had he known that such a gabbling flock of popinjays were on the wing thither!"

But the young gallants were chiefly bent on speculating on the vision of loveliness that had flashed on the eyes of some early visitants at the well. A maiden in a dark pilgrim dress, and broad hat, which, however, could not entirely conceal a glowing complexion, at once rich and pure; perfect features, magnificent dark eyes and hair, and a tall form, which, though very youthful, was of unmistakable dignity and grace. She was always at the well exceedingly early in the morning, moving slowly round it on her beautiful bare feet, and never looking up from the string of dark beads—the larger ones of amber, which she held in her fingers—as her lips conned over the prayers connected with each. No ring was on the delicate hand, no ear-ring in the ear; there was no ornament in the dress, but such a garb was wont to be assumed by ladies of any rank when performing a vow; and its simplicity at once enhanced her beauty, and added to the general curiosity. Between four and six in the dewy freshness of morning seemed to be her time for devotion; and though the habits of the court were early, it was only the first astir who caught a sight of this Queen of the Dew-drops, as it was the fashion to call her. Late comers never caught sight of her, and affected incredulity when the younger and more active knights and squires raved about her. Then it was reported that the King himself had been seen speaking to her; and thereupon excitement grew the more intense, because Edward's exclusive devotion to his Queen had been such, that from his youth up the most determined scandal had never found a wandering glance to note in him.

She was the Princess of France—of Navarre—of Aragon—in disguise; nay, at the Whit-Sunday banquet there were those who cast anxious glances to the door, expecting that, in the very land of King Arthur, she would walk in like his errant dames at Pentecost, to demand a champion. And when a joust was given on the sward, young Sir John de Mohun, the Lord of Dunster, announced his intention of tilting in honour of no one save the Queen of the Dew-drops. The ladies of the court were rather scandalized, and appealed to the King whether the choice of an unknown girl, of no acknowledged rank, should be permitted; but the King, strict punctilious man as he was, only laughed, and adjudged the Queen of the Dew-drops to be fully worthy of the honour.

After this, early rising became the fashion of Holy-well. All the gentlemen got up early to look at the Queen of the Dew-drops; and all the ladies got up early to see that the gentlemen did not get into mischief; and the maiden's devotions became far from solitary; but she moved on, with a sort of superb unconcern, never lifting the dark fringes that veiled the eyes so steadily fixed on the beads that dropped through her fingers, until, as she finished, she raised up her head with a straightforward fearless look at the way she was going, so completely self-possessed that no one ventured to accost her, and to follow her at less than such a respectful distance, that she was always lost sight of in the wood.

At last, late one evening, there was a sudden start of exultant satisfaction among some of the young men who were lounging on the green; for the most part not the nobles of the court, but certain young merchants of London and Bristol, who had followed the course of pilgrimage by the magnetism of fashionable resort. The Queen of the Dew-drops was seen, carrying a pitcher! Up started four or five gallants, offering assistance, and standing round her, wrangling with one another, and besetting her steps.

"Let me pass, gentles," she said with dignity, "I am carrying wine in haste to my father."

"Nay, fair one, you pass not our bounds without toll," said the portliest of the set.

"Hush, rudesby; fair dames in disguise must be treated after other sort."

Every variety of half-insulting compliment was pouring upon her; but she, with head erect, and steady foot, still quietly moved on, taking no notice, till a hand was laid on her pitcher.

"Let go!" then she said in no terrified voice. "Let go, Sir, or I can summon help."

And as if to realize her words, the intrusive hand was thrust aside by a powerful arm, and a voice exclaimed -

"This lady is to pass free, Sir! None of your insolence!"

"A court-gallant," passed round the hostile bourgeoise; "none of your court airs, Sir."

"No airs—but those of an honest Englishman, who will not see a woman cowardly beset!"

"Will Silk-jerkin not bide a buffet!" quoth the bully of the party, clenching his fist.

"As many as thou wilt," returned Silk-jerkin, "so soon as I have seen the lady safe home!"

"Ho! ho!—a fetch that!" and the fellow, a coarse rude-looking man, though rather expensively dressed, flourished his fist in the face of the young man, but was requited that instant with a round blow that levelled him with the ground. The others fell back from the tall strong-limbed, open-faced youth, and the girl took the opportunity of moving forward, swiftly indeed, but so steadily as to betray no air of terror. Meantime, the young gentleman's voice might be heard, assuring his adversaries that he was ready to encounter one or all of them so soon as he had escorted the lady safe home. Perhaps she hoped that another attack would delay him; but if so, her expectations were disappointed, for in a second or two his quick firm tread followed her, and just as she had gained the mazy wood-path, he was beside her.

"Thanks, Sir," she said, "for the service you have done me, but I am now in safety."

"Nay, Lady, do me the grace of letting me bear your load."

"Thanks," again she said; "but I feel no weight."

"But my knighthood does, seeing you thus laden."

"Spare your knighthood the sight, then," she said smiling, and looking up with a glance of brightness, such as her hitherto sedate face had never before revealed to him.

"That cannot be!" he exclaimed with fervency. "You bid me in vain leave you till I see you safe; and while with you, all laws of courtesy call on me to bear your burthen! So, Lady—"

And he laid his hand upon the leathern thong that sustained the pitcher; but at that moment three or four heaps of rags, that had been lying under the trees by the woodland path, erected themselves, and one in especial, whom the young knight had observed as a frightful cripple seated by day near the well, now came forward brandishing his crutch in a formidable manner, and uttering a howl of defiance. But the lady silenced him at once -

"Peace, good Trig, nothing is amiss! It is only this gentleman's courtesy. He hath done me good service on the green yonder!"

And as her strange body-guard retreated growling, she, perhaps to show her confidence, resigned her pitcher into the knight's hand.

"So, fair Queen of the Dew-drops," he said, half bewildered, "thou dost work miracles!"

"Ay, when the dew is on the grass, and the nightingale sings," she returned gaily; "by day the enchantment is over."

By this time they had reached a low turf hut; and the maiden, turning at the door, held out her hand, and said, "Thanks, fair Sir, I must enter my enchanted palace alone; but grammercy for thy kind service, and farewell."

The maiden and the pitcher vanished. The knight watched the rude door in vain—he only saw a few streaks of light through the boards. Then he bethought him of questioning her guards, but when he reached their tree they were gone. It was fast growing dark, and he was one of the King's personal attendants, and subject to the strict regulations of his household; so, dazed and bewildered as he was, he walked hastily back to the hospice, where the King and Queen lodged. Supper had already begun, and the glare of lights dazzled his eyes. In his bewilderment, he served the King with mustard instead of honey from the great silver ship full of condiments, in the centre of the table.

"How's this, Sir John?" said the King, who always had a kindly corner in his heart for this young knight. "Are these the idle days of thy Crusade come again?"

"I could well-nigh think so!" half-whispered Sir John.

"He looks moonstruck!" cried that spoilt ten years old damsel, Joan of Acre, clasping her hands with mischievous fun. "Oh! has he seen the Queen of the Dew-drops?"

"What dost thou know of the Queen of the Dew-drops, my Lady Malapert?" said King Edward, marking the red flush that mounted to the very brow of the downright young knight.

"Oh, I know that she is at the well every morning, and is as lovely as the dawn! Ay, and vanishes so soon as the sun is up; but not ere she has bewitched every knight of them all! And did not my Lord of Dunster hold the field in her honour against all comers? No wonder she appears to him.—Oh! tell us, Sir John! what like was she?"

"Hush, Joan," said Queen Eleanor, bending forward, "no infanta in my time ever said so much in a breath."

"No, Lady-mother; because you had to speak whole mouthfuls of grave Castillian words. Now, good English can be run off in a breath. Reyna del Rocio—that's more majestic, but not so like fairyland as Queen of the Dew-drops!"

Princess Joan's mouth was effectually stopped this time.

The adventure of the evening had led to the discovery of the hut of the Queen of the Dew-drops. The young knight had as usual been betimes at the well, but the maiden did not appear there. Then he questioned the cripple—who by day was an absolute helpless cripple— but the man utterly denied all knowledge of any such circumstance. He, why, poor wretch that he was, he never hobbled further than the shed close behind the well; he would give the world if he could get as far as the wood—he knew nothing about ladies or pilgrims—such a leg as his was enough to think about. And the display to which he forthwith treated the Knight of Dunster was highly convincing as to his incapacity.

Into the wood wandered the much-confused knight, recognizing, step by step, the path of the night before. The turf hut was before him—the door was open —and in the doorway sat the maiden herself, spinning, the distaff by her side, the spindle dancing on the ground, and the pilgrim's hat no longer hiding her beauteous brow and wealth of dark braided hair. But, intolerable sight, seven or eight of last night's loungers were dispersed hither and thither in the bushes, gazing with all their eyes, endeavouring to attract her attention; some by conversations with one another; one richly-dressed Gascon squire, of the train of Edward's ally, the Count de Bearn, by singing a Provencal love ditty; while a merchant of Bristol set up a counter attempt with a long doleful English ballad. All the time the fair spinster sat in the doorway, with the utmost gravity, twisting her thread and twirling her spindle; but it might be observed that she had so placed herself as to have full command of the door, and to be able to shut herself in whenever she chose.

No one had yet ventured to accost her. There was something in her air that rendered it almost impossible for any one to force himself upon her, and a sort of fear mingled with the impression she made. However, the young knight, although a bashful man by nature, had one advantage in his court breeding, and another in the acquaintance he had made last night. He walked straight up, and doffing his velvet cap, began, "Greet you well, fair Queen. I could not but take your challenge to see whether your power lasted when the dew was off."

The damsel rose with due courtesy as he approached, but ere she had attempted an answer, nay, even before the words were out of his mouth, the Gascon was shouting in French that this was no fair play, he had stolen a march; and the merchant had sprung forward saying, "Girl, beware, court gallants mean not well by country wenches."

"Thou liest in thy throat," burst forth the knight. "Discourteous lubber, to call such a queen of beauty a country wench!"

"Listen to me, girl."

"Lady, hear me."

"Hearken not to the popinjay foreigner."

These, and many more tumultuary exclamations, threats, and entreaties, crowded on one another, and the various speakers were laying hand on staff or sword, and glaring angrily on one another, when the word "Peace," in the maiden's clear silvery notes, sounded among them. They all turned as she stood in the doorway, drawn up to her full height.

"Peace," she said; "I can have no brawling here! My father was grievously sick yesterday, and is still ill at ease. One by one speak your business, and begone. You first, Sir," to the Gascon, she said in French.

"Ah! fair Lady, what business could be mine, save to tell you how lovely you are?"

"You have said," she answered, without a blush, waving him aside. "Now you, Sir," to the tuneful merchant of Bristol.

"I told you, Madam, he meant not well. Those aliens never do."

"You too have said," she answered.

The merchant would have persisted, but a London merchant, a much more substantial and considerable character, pushed him aside, and the numbers being all against him, he was forced to give way.

"Young woman," said the merchant, "you are plainly of better birth and breeding than you choose to affect. Now I am thinking of getting married. I have ships at sea, and stuffs and jewels coming from Venice and Araby; and I am like to be Lord Mayor ere long; but there's that I like in your face and discreet bearing, and I'll make you my wife, and give you all my keys—your father willing!"

"Your turn's out, old burgher," said a big, burly, and much younger man, pressing forward. "Pretty wench! I'm not like to be Lord Mayor, nor nothing of that sort; but I'm a score of years nigher thine age, and a lusty fellow to boot, that could floor any man at single-stick, within the four seas. Ay, and have been thought comely too, though Joyce o' the haugh did play me false; and I come o' this pilgrimage just to be merry and forget it. If thou wilt take me, and come back to spite Joyce, thou shalt be hostess of the Black Bull, at Brentford, where all the great folk from the North ever put up when they come to town; the merriest and richest hostel, and will have the comeliest host and hostess round about London town!"

The lady bowed her head. Perhaps those rosy lips were trying hard to keep from laughing.

"A hostel's no place for a discreet dame to bide in," put forth an honest voice. "Maiden, I know not who or what you are, but I came o' this pilgrimage to please my old mother, who said I might do my soul good, and bring home a wife—better over the moor than over the mixen—and I know she would give thee a right good welcome. I'm Baldric of the Cheddar Cliff, and we have held our land ever since the old days, or ever the Norman kings came here. Three hundred kine, woman, and seven score swine, and many an acre of good corn land under the hill."

The lady had never looked up while these suitors were speaking. When Baldric of Cheddar had done, she gave one furtive glance through her long eyelashes, as if to see if there were any more, and then her cheek flushed. There still remained the knight. Some others had slunk away when brought to such close quarters, but he stepped forth more hesitatingly, and said, "Lady, I know not whether the bare rock and castle I have to offer can weigh against the ships, the hostel, or the swine. I have few of either; I am but a poor baron, but such as I am, I am wholly yours. Thine eyes have bound me to you for ever, and all I seek is leave to make myself better known, and to ask that your noble father may not deem me wholly unworthy to be your suitor."

The lady trembled a little, but she held her place in the doorway. "Gentles," she said, "I thank ye for the honour ye have done me, but I may not dispose of mine own self. My father is ill at ease, and can see no one; but he bids me tell you that he will meet all who have aught to say to him, under the trysting tree at Bethnal Green, the day after the Midsummer feast."

With these words she retired into her hut, and closed the door. She was seen again no more that day; and on the next the hut stood open, empty, and deserted.

CHAPTER XV—THE BEGGAR'S DOWRY

"'But first you shall promise and have it well knowne
The gold that you drop shall all be your owne;'
With that they replyed, 'Contented we bee;'
'Then here's,' quoth the beggar, 'for pretty Bessee.'"
Old Ballad.

The day after Midsummer had come, and towards the fine elm tree that then adorned the centre of Bethnal Green, three horsemen were wending their way. Each had his steed a good deal loaded: each looked about him anxiously.

"By St. Boniface," said one, "the girl's father is not there. Saucy little baggage, was she deluding us all?"

"Belike he is bringing too long a train of mules with her dowry to make much speed," quoth the merchant. "He will think it needful to collect all his gear to meet the offers of Master Lambert of Cripple- gate. Ha! Sir Knight, well met! You are going to try your venture!"

"I must! So it were not all enchantment," said the knight, almost breathlessly, gazing round him. "Yet," he said, almost to himself, "those eyes had a soul and memories that ne'er came out of fairyland!"

"Ha!" exclaimed the innkeeper, "there's old Blind Hal under the tree! I'll tell him to get out of our way. Hal!" he shouted, "here's a tester for thee, but thou'st best keep out of the way of the mules."

"What mules, Master Samson?" coolly demanded Hal, who had comfortably established himself under the tree with his back against the trunk.

"The mules that the brave burgess is going to bring his daughter's dowry on. They are cranky brutes, Hal; bad customers for blind men— best let me give thee a hand out of the way."

"But who is this burgess that you talk of?" asked the beggar.

"The father of the pilgrim lass that prayed at St. Winifred's Well," said Samson.

"And was called Queen of the Dew-drops?"

"Ay, ay, old fellow! Thou knowest every bird that flies! She is to be my wife, I tell thee, and a right warm corner shall she keep for thee at the Black Bull, for thou canst make sport for the guests right well."

"I hope she will keep a warm corner for me," said the beggar; "for no man will treat for her marriage save myself."

"Thou! Old man, who sent thee here to insult us?" cried the merchant.

"None, Master Lambert. I trysted you to meet me here if you purposed still to seek my child in marriage."

"Thy child?" cried all three, vehemently.

"My child!" answered the beggar. "Mine own lawful child."

There was a silence. Presently Samson growled, "I mind me he used to have a little black-eyed brat with him."

"Caitiff!" exclaimed the merchant; "I'll have thy old vagabond bones in the Fleet for daring so to cheat his Grace's lieges."

"If you can prove a cheat against me I will readily abye it, Sir," returned the beggar.

"Palming a beggar's brat off for a noble dame."

"So please you, Sir," interrupted the beggar, "keep truth with you. What did the child or I ever profess, save what we were? No foul words here. I trysted you to meet me here, anent her marriage. Have you any offers to make me?"

"Aye, of a cell in the Fleet if you persist in your insolence!" cried the merchant.

"Thanks," quietly said the beggar. "And you, Master Samson?"

"'Tis a sweet pretty lass," said Samson, ruefully; "and pity of her too, but you see a man like me must look to his credit. I'll give her twenty marks to help her to a husband, Hal, only let her keep out of my sight for ever and a day."

"I thought I heard another voice," said the beggar. "I trow the third suitor has made off without further ado."

"Not so, fair Sir," said a voice close to him, thick and choked with feeling. "Your daughter is too dear to me for me thus to part, even were mine honour not pledged."

"Sir knight," interfered the merchant, "you will get into a desperate coil with your friends."

"I am my own master," answered the knight. "My parents are dead. I am of age, and, Sir, I offer myself and all that is mine to your fair daughter, as I did at Saint Winifred's Well, as one bound both by honour and love."

"It is spoken honourably," said Hal; "but, Sir, canst thou answer me with her dowry? Tell down coin for coin."

He held up a heavy leathern bag. The knight, who had come prepared, took down another such bag from his saddle-bow. Down went one silver piece from the knight. Down went another from the beggar.

"Stay, stay," cried Samson. "I can play at that game too."

"No, no, Master Samson," said the beggar; "your pretensions are resigned. Your chance is over."

Mark after mark—crown after crown—all the Dunster rents; all the old hoards, with queer figures of Saxon kings, lay on the grass, still for each the beggar had rained down its fellow, and inexhaustible seemed the bags that he sat upon. Samson bit his lips, and the merchant muttered with vexation. It could not be fairly come by: he must be the president of a den of robbers; it should be looked to.

The last bag of the knight lay thin and exhausted; the beggar clutched one bursting with repletion.

"I could not put the lands and castle of Dunster into a bag and add thereto," said the knight, at last. "Would that I could, my sword, my spurs, and knightly blood to boot, and lay them at your daughter's feet."

"Let them weigh in the balance," said the beggar; "and therewith thy truth to thy word."

"And will you own me?" exclaimed the knight. "Will you take me to your daughter?"

"Nay, I said not so," returned Blind Hal. "I am not in such haste. Come back on this day week, when I shall have learnt whether thou art worthy to match with my child."

"Worthy!" John of Dunster chafed and bit his lips at such words from a beggar.

"Ay, worthy," repeated the beggar, guessing his irritation. "I like thee well, as a man of thy word, so far, but I must know more of him who is to mate with my pretty Bessee."

It was that evening that a page entered the royal apartments, and giving a ring to the King, informed him that a blind beggar had sent it in, and entreated to speak with him.

"Pray him to come hither," said the King; "and lead him carefully. Thou, Joan, hadst better seek thy mother and sister."

"O sweet father," cried Joan, "don't order me off. This can be no state business. Prithee let me hear it."

"That must be as my guest pleases, Joan," he answered; "and thou must be very discreet, or we shall have him reproaching me for trying to rule the realm when I cannot rule my own house."

"Father, I verily think you are afraid of that beggar! I am sure he is as mysterious as the Queen of the Dew-drops!" cried the mischievous girl.

The curtain over the doorway was drawn back, and the beggar was led into the chamber. The King advanced to meet him, and took his hand to lead him to a seat. "Good morrow to thee," he said; "cousin, I am glad thou art come at last to see me."

"Thanks, my Lord," said the beggar, with more of courtly tone than when they had met before, and yet Joan thought she had never seen her father addressed so much as an equal; "are any here present with you?"

"Only my wilful little crusading daughter, Joan," said Edward, beckoning to her, and putting her proud reluctant fingers into the hand of the beggar, who bent and raised them to his lips—as the fashion then was—while the maiden reddened and looked to her father, but saw him only smiling; "she shall leave us," he added, "if thy matters are for my private ear. In what can I aid thee?"

"In this matter of daughters," answered the beggar; "not that I need aid of yours, but counsel. I would know if the heir of old Reginald Mohun—John, I think they call him—be a worthy mate for my wench."

Joan had in the meantime placed herself between her father's knees, where she stood regarding this wonderful beggar with the most unmitigated astonishment.

"John of Dunster!" said the King, stroking down Joan's hair, "thou knowst his lineage as well as I, cousin."

"His lineage, true," replied Henry; "but look you, my Lord, my child, the light of mine eyes, may not go from me without being assured that it is to one who will, I say, not equal her in birth, but will be a faithful and loving lord to her."

"Hath he sought her?" asked the King.

"Even so, my liege. The maid is scarce sixteen; I thought to have kept her longer; but so it was—old Winny, her mother's old nurse, fell sick and died in the winter; and the Dominican, who came to shrive her, must needs craze the poor fool with threats that she did a deadly sin in bringing my sweet wife and me together; and for all the Grand Prior, who, monk as he is, has a soldier's sense, could say of the love that conquered death, nothing would serve the poor woman to die in peace till my Bessee had vowed to make a six weeks' station at her patroness's well, where we were wedded, and pray for her soul and her blessed mother's. So there we journeyed for our summer roaming; and all had been well, had you not come down on us with all the idle danglers of the court to gaze and rhyme and tilt about the first fair face they saw. Even then so discreet was the girl that no more had befallen, but as ill-luck would have it, my old Evesham keepsake," touching his side, "burst forth again one evening, and left me so spent, that Bessee sent the boy to get me a draught of wine. The boy—mountebank as he is—lost her groat, and played truant; and she, poor wench, got into such fear for me that she went herself, and fell in with a sort of insolent masterful rogues, from whom this young knight saved her. I took her home safe enough after that, and thought to be rid of the knaves when they saw my wallet; and so truly I am, all save this lad!"

"O father! it is true love!" whispered Joan.

"What hast to do with true love, popinjay? And so John of Dunster came undaunted to the breach, did he, Henry?"

"Not a whit dismayed he! Now either that is making light of his honour, or 'tis an honour higher than most lads understand. Cousin, I would have the child be loved as her father and mother loved! And methinks she affects this blade. The child hath been less like my merry lark since we met him. A plague on the springalds! But you know him. Has he your good word?"

"John of Dunster?" said the King. "Henry, didst thou not know for whose sake I had loved and proved him? He was Richard's pupil. I was forced to take the child with me, for old Sir Reginald had been unruly enough, and I thought would be the less troublesome to my father were his son in my keeping. But I half repented when I saw what a small urchin it was, to be cast about among grooms and pages! But Richard aided the little uncouth varlet, nursed him when sick, guarded him when well, trained him to be loyal and steadfast. The little fellow came bravely to my aid in my grapple with the traitor before Acre; and when the blow had fallen on Richard, the boy's grief was such that I loved him ever after. And of late I have had no truer trustier warrior. I warrant me he was too shy to tell thee that I knighted him last year in the midst of some of the best feats of arms I ever beheld against the Welsh! Whatever John de Mohun saith is sooth, and I would rather mate my daughter with him than with many a man of fairer speech."

"Then shall he have my pretty Bessee!" said the beggar, lingering over the words. "But one boon I would further ask, cousin; that thou breathe no word to him of my having sought thee."

The young Lord of Dunster had not been noted for choiceness of apparel; but when he repaired to the trysting-tree, none could have found fault with the folds of his long crimson tunic, worked with the black and gold colours of his family, nor with the sit of the broad belt that sustained his sword, assuredly none with his beautiful sleek black charger.

But under the tree stood not the blind beggar, but the beggar's boy.

"Blind Hal bids you meet him at the Spital, at your good pleasure," said the boy; and like the mountebank he was, tumbled three times head over heels.

John de Mohun looked round and about, and saw no alternative but to obey. All his love was required to endure so strange a father-in- law, who did not seem in the least grateful for the honour intended to his daughter; but the knight's word was pledged, and he rode towards the Hospital.

The court of the Hospital was full of steeds and serving-men. A strange conviction came over John that he saw the King's strong white charger—ay, and the palfreys of the elder princesses; and he asked the lay-brother who offered to take his horse, if the King were there. The brother only replied by motioning him towards the inner quadrangle.

He passed on accordingly, and as he went, the bells broke forth into a merry peal. On the top of the steps leading to the arched doorway, he saw a scarlet cluster of knights, and among them the Grand Prior, robed as for Mass. A space was clear within the deep porch, and there stood the beggar in his russet suit.

"Sir John de Mohun of Dunster," he said, "thou art come hither to espouse my daughter?"

"I hope, so, Sir," said John, somewhat taken by surprise.

"Come hither, maiden," said her father.

The cluster of knights opened, and from within the church there appeared before the astonished bridegroom the stately form of King Edward, leading in his hand the dark-tressed, dark-haired maiden, dressed in spotless white, the only adornment she wore a circlet of diamonds round her flowing dark hair—the Queen indeed of the Dew- drops. And behind her walked with calm dignity the beautiful Princess Eleanor, now nearly a woman, holding with a warning hand the merry mischievous Joan.

Well might John of Dunster stand dazzled and amazed, but hesitation or delay there was none. Then and there, by the Grand Prior himself, was the ceremony performed, without a word of further explanation. The rite over, when the bridegroom took the bride's hand to follow, as all were marshalled on their way, he knew not whither, she looked up to him through her dark eyelashes, and murmured, "They would not have it otherwise!"

"Deem you that I would?" said the knight fervently, pressing her hand.

"I deemed that you should know all—who I am," she faltered.

"My wife, the Lady of Dunster. That is all I need to know," replied Sir John, with the honest trustworthy look that showed it was indeed enough to secure his heart-whole love and reverence.

The great hall of the Spital was decked for the bridal feast. The bride and bridegroom were placed at the head of the table, and the King gave up his place beside the bride to her blind father. All the space within the cloister without was strewn with rushes, where sat and feasted the whole fraternity of beggars; and well did the Grand Prior and his knights do their part in the entertainment.

Then when the banquet was drawing to its close, the blind beggar bade the boy that waited near him fetch his harp. And, as had often before been his practice, he sang in a deep manly voice, to the boy's accompaniment on his harp. But the song that then he sang had never been heard before, nor was its exact like ever heard again; though tradition has handed down a few of the main features, and (as may be seen by this veracious narration) somewhat vulgarized them:-

"A poore beggar's daughter did dwell on a greene,
Who might for her faireness have well been a queene;
A blithe bonny lasse and a dainty was she,
And many one called her pretty Bessee."

Even the King, who had so well guarded the secret, was entirely unprepared to hear the Montfort parentage thus publicly avowed; and the bride, who had as little known of her father's intentions, sat with downcast eyes, blushing and tearful, while the beggar's recitative went briefly and somewhat tremulously over his resuscitation, under the hands of the fair and faithful Isabel. Her hand was held by her bridegroom from the first, with a pressure meant to assure her that no discovery could alter his love and regard; but when the name of Montfort sounded on his ear, the hand wrung hers with anxiety; and when the entire tale had been told, and the last chord was dying away, he murmured, "Look up at me, my loveliest. Now I know why I first loved thine eyes. Thou art dearer to me than ever, for the sake of my first and best friend!"

His words were only for herself. The King was saying aloud,

"Well sung, fair cousin! A health, my Lords and Knights, for Sir Henry de Montfort, Earl of Leicester."

"Not so, Lords and Knights!" called this strange personage, the only one who would thus have contradicted the King; "the Earl of Leicester has long ago been dead, as you have heard. If you drink, let it be to Blind Hal of Bethnal Green."

Nor could all the entreaties of daughter, son-in-law, nor King, move him from his purpose of living and dying as Blind Hal, the beggar. He had tasted too long of liberty, he said, to put himself under constraint. To live in Somersetshire, as his daughter wished, would have been banishment and solitude to one used to divert himself with every humour of the city; and to be, as he declared, a far more complete king of the beggars than ever his cousin Edward was over England. All he would consent to, was that a room in a lodge in Windsor Park should be set apart for him under charge of Adam de Gourdon, who had been present at this scene, and was infinitely rejoiced at the sight of a scion of the House of Montfort. For the rest, he bade every one to forget his avowal, which, as he said, he had only made that the blanch lion might share with the Mohun cross; and as he added to Princess Eleanor, "that you court dames may never flout at pretty Bessee! Had the Cheddar Yeoman been the true man, none had ever known that she was a Montfort."

"Would you have given her to the Cheddar Yeoman?" burst out Joan furiously.

"That he will say so, to anger thee, is certain, Joan," said the King. "Farewell, Henry. Remember, I hold thee bound to be my comrade when I can return to the Holy War."

"Ay, when you have tamed Scotland, even as you have tamed Wales," returned Henry.

"No fear of my good brother Alexander's realm needing such taming. Heaven forbid!" said Edward.

But the beggar parted from him with a laugh.

CHAPTER XVI—THE PAGE'S MEMORY

The pure calm picture of a blameless friend.
Lyra Apostolica.

Ten years later, King Edward was walking in the park at Windsor with slow and weary steps. His rich dark brown hair and beard were lined with gray, his face was not only grave but worn and melancholy, and more severe than ever. The sorrow of his life, his queen's death, had fallen on him, and with her had gone much of softening influence; the only son who had been spared to him was, though a mere child, grieving him by the wayward frivolities not of a strong but of a weak nature; he had wrought much for his country's good, but had often been thwarted and never thanked; his mercies and benefits were forgotten, his justice counted as harshness, and hatred and opposition had met him everywhere. Above all, and weighting him perhaps most severely, was that his first step beyond his just bounds had been taken in the North. John Baliol was indeed king, but Edward in his zeal for discipline had bound Scotland with obligations—for her good indeed, but beyond his just right to impose; and the sense of aggression was embittering him against the Scottish resistance, while at the same time adding to his sadness.

A knight came forth from one of the paths that led into that along which he was pacing with folded arms, and unwilling to break upon his mood, stood waiting, till Edward himself looked up and asked impatiently, "So, Sir John, what now? Another outbreak of those intolerable Scotch?"

"Not so, my Lord; but the Bailiff of Acre awaits to see you."

"Bailiff of Acre! What is the Bailiff of Acre to me? I cannot hear all their importunities for a crusade! Heaven knows how gladly I would hasten to the Holy War, if these savage Scots would give me peace at home. I am weary of their solicitations. Cannot you tell him I would be private, John?"

"My Lord, he says he has matter for your private ear, concerning one whom you met in Palestine—and, my Lord, you will sure remember him— Sir Reginald Ferrers."

"The friend of Richard!" said Edward, with a changed countenance. "Bring him with you to your father-in-law's lodge, John. If there be aught to hear of the House of Montfort, it concerns him and you likewise. I was on my way thither."

In a short time the woodland lodge, in one of the most beautiful glades of Windsor Forest, beheld the King seated on a bench placed beneath a magnificent oak, standing alone in its own glade, and beside him the Blind Beggar in his russet suit; far less changed than his royal cousin during these years. Since Edward's great sorrow, Henry de Montfort had held less apart from him; and whenever the King was at leisure to snatch a short retirement at one of his hunting lodges, he always sent an intimation to the beggar, who would journey down on a sober ass, and under the care of De Gourdon, now the chief of the hunting staff, would meet the King in some sylvan glade. Why it was a comfort to Edward to be with him, it would be hard to say; probably from the habit of old fellowship, for Henry's humour had not grown more courtly or less caustic.

From under the trees came John de Mohun, now a brave, stout, hearty-looking English baron; and with him, wrapped in a battered and soiled scarlet mantle, a war-worn soldier, his complexion tanned to deep brown, his hair bleached with toil and sun, a scar on his cheek, a halt on his step—altogether a man in whom none would have recognized the bright, graceful, high-spirited young Hospitalier of twenty years since. Only when he spoke, and the smiling light beamed in his eye, could he be known for Sir Reginald Ferrers.

He would have bent his knee, but Edward took his hand, and bowing his own bared head said, "It is we who should crave a blessing from you, holy Father, last defender of the sacred land."

"Alas, my Lord," said Sir Raynald, as he made the gesture of blessing; "Heaven's will he done! Had we but been worthier! Sir," he added, "I am in no guise for a royal presence, but I have been sent home from Cyprus to recover from my wounds; and I had a message for you which I deemed you would gladly hear before I had joined mine Order."

"A message?" said Edward.

"A message from a dying penitent, craving pardon," replied Sir Raynald.

"If it concerns the House of Montfort, speak on," said Edward. "None are so near to it as those present with me!"

"Thou hast guessed right, my Lord King!" replied Sir Raynald. "It does concern that House. Have I your license to tell my tale at some length?"

Edward gave permission; and a seat having been brought, Sir Raynald proceeded to speak of that last Siege of Acre, when, amid the multitudinous tribunals of mixed races, and the many sanctuaries which sheltered crime, the unhappy city had become a disgrace to the Christian name. The Sultan Malek Seraf was concentrating his forces on it; all the unwarlike inhabitants had been sent away; and the Knights of the two Orders, with the King of Cyprus and his troops, had shut themselves up for their last resistance—when among the mercenaries, who enrolled themselves in the pay of the Hospitaliers, came a sunburnt warrior, who had evidently had long experience of Eastern warfare, though his speech was English, French, or Provencal, according to the person who addressed him. Fierce and dreadful was the daily strife; the new soldier fought well, but he was not noticed, till one night. "Ah, Sir!" said the Hospitalier, "even then our holy and beautiful house was in dire confusion, our garden trodden down and desolate! One night, I heard strange choking sobs as of one in anguish. I deemed that one of our wounded had in delirium wandered into the garden, and was dying there. But I found- -at the foot of the stone cross we set beside the fountain, where the attempt on you, Sir, was made—this warrior lying, so writhing with anguish, that I could scarce believe it was grief, not pain, that thus wrought with him! I lifted him up, and spake of repentance and pardon. No pardon for him, he said; it was here that he had slain his brother! I spake long and earnestly with him, but he called himself sacrilegious murderer again and again. Nay, he had even— when after that wretched night you wot of, Sir, he left our House—in his despair and hope to leave remorse behind, he had become a Moslem, and fought in the Saracen ranks. All hope he spurned. No mercy for him, was his cry! I would have deemed so—but oh! I thought of Richard's parting hope; I remembered our German brethren's tale, how the Holy Father, the Pope, said there was as little hope of pardon as that his staff should bud and blossom; and lo, in one night it bore bud and flower. I besought him for Richard's sake to let me strive in prayer for him. All day we fought on the walls—all night, beside Richard's cross, did he lie and weep and groan, and I would pray till strength failed both of us. Day after day, night after night, and still the miserable man looked gray with despair, and still he told me that he knew Absolution would but mock his doom. He could fear, but could not sorrow. And still I spoke of the Saviour's love of man—and still I prayed, and all our house prayed with me, though they knew not who the sinner was for whom I besought their prayers. At last—it was the day when the towers on the walls had been won—I came back from the breach, and scarce rested to eat bread, ere I went on to the Cedar and the Cross. Beside it knelt Sir Simon. 'Father,' he said, 'I trust that the pardon that takes away the sin of the world, will take away mine. Grant me Absolution.' He was with us when, ere dawn, such of us as still lived met for our last mass in our beautiful chapel. He went forth with us to the wall. By and by, the command was given that we should make a sally upon the enemy's camp. We went back for the last time to our house to fetch our horses; I knew there could be no return, and went for one last look into our chapel, and at Richard's tomb. Upon it lay the knight, horribly scathed with Greek fire—he had dragged him there to die. He was dead, but his looks were upward; his face was as calm as Richard's was, my Lord, when we laid him down by the fountain. And now his message, my Lord. He bade me say, if I survived the siege, that he had often cursed you for the worse revenge of letting him live to his remorse—now he blessed you for sparing him to repent."

"And Richard's grave has passed to the Infidels!" said Edward, after a long silence.

"Even as the graves of our brethren—the holiest Grave of all," said the Knight Hospitalier.

"Cheer up and hope, Father," said the King. "Let me see peace and order at home, and we will win back Acre, ay and Jerusalem, from the Infidels. Alas! our young hopes and joys may never return; but, home purified, then may God bless our arms beneath the Cross."

Fifteen years more, and in the beautiful Westminster Abbey, amid the gorgeous tombs, there stood four sorrowful figures. A sturdy knight, with bowed head and mournful look, carefully guided a white-haired, white-bearded old man, while a beautiful matronly lady was handed by her tall handsome son.

Among the richly inlaid shrines and monuments, they sought out one the latest of all, but consisting of one enormous block of stone, with no ornament save one slender band of inscription.

"Ah!" said the knight, "well do I remember the shipping of that stone from Acre, little guessing its purpose!"

"Then it is indeed a stone from the ruined Temple of Jerusalem," said the lady. "Read the inscription, my Son."

The young man read and translated -

"Edwardus Primus. Malleus Scotorum Pactum serva.
Edward the First. The Hammer of the Scots. Keep covenant."

"It was scarce worth while to bring a stone from Jerusalem, to mark it with 'the Hammer of the Scots!'" said the lady.

"Alas, my cousin Edward!" sighed the beggar. "Ever with a great scheme, ever going earnestly on to its fulfilment; with a mind too far above those of other men to be understood or loved as thou shouldst have been! Alack, that the Scottish temptation came between thee and the brightness of thy glory! Art thou indeed gone—like Richard—to Jerusalem; and shall I yet follow thee there? Let us pray for the peace of his soul, children; for a greater and better man lies here than England knows or heeds."

Footnotes:

{1} Psalm cxxvi. 6, 7.

www.ingramcontent.com/pod-product-compliance
Lightning Source LLC
Chambersburg PA
CBHW020022030726
47499CB00007B/2229